EVERYTHING SHE NEEDED

A CEDAR VALLEY NOVEL

CHRISTINA BUTRUM

Welcome Back! ♥

♥ Christina
Butrum

ALSO BY CHRISTINA BUTRUM

FAIRSHORE SERIES

Second Chances

Unexpected Chances

Fair Chances

CEDAR VALLEY SERIES

All She Ever Wanted

Everything She Needed

KATE'S DUET

Kate's Valentine

Kate's Forever

No Place Like Home: Love in Seattle

ACKNOWLEDGMENTS

With this being my eighth published book, you would think that I would be a pro at writing the acknowledgments...not even close...But here goes my best attempt at thanking those who make this possible for me each and every day.

My readers - Without you, who else would fall in love with my characters? They need you. Thank you for taking a chance on a new author.

Betas - You continue to provide valuable feedback with each and every book I send your way. Thank you!

Amanda Walker - aka Cover Queen - I enjoy working with you! You're one heck of a cover designer and I love your attention to detail. You provide me with so much, that I'm forever thankful for you and our friendship.

My editor, Janet at Dragonfly Editing - I can never thank you enough! You're one of a kind and I'm thankful I have you to edit my errors.

Fellow authors who have become good friends of mine - It amazes me how lost one can get in this Indie

World, but I have nothing to worry about when I have all of you in my corner. Thank you for always being there.

Nate, Alaina, my parents, and other family who continue to support me in this dream of mine to write full time someday - Thank you! Your support and encouragement means the world to me!

XOXO - Christina

Edited By: Dragonfly Editing

Cover By: Amanda Walker PA & Design Services

❀ Created with Vellum

To my readers who fell in love with Cedar Valley.

The mountains in the distance guided her home. Leah had been right since day one—there was something about Cedar Valley that encouraged everyone to come back, settle down, and call it home.

*A*va babbled along to a Sesame Street movie in the backseat as they headed west to Cedar Valley. It had taken longer than Rachel had planned to get all of their things loaded into the car. Renting a U-Haul had crossed her mind, but with the help of Adam and his friends, the majority of her stuff had arrived in Cedar Valley last week. All that was left was packed in separate totes and strategically placed in the rear end of her car.

Leaving the city had been tough, but with her relationship with Adam progressing further than it had within the last year, she had decided it was time for her and Ava to take the venture and accept what may come.

The sun set just beyond the mountains, giving the sky a shade of rose petal pink with a hint of lavender and honey. There was something about the setting sun and the highway guiding her way to Cedar Valley. It just felt right.

Cedar Valley had a lot to offer, including the main reason for her move with Ava, Adam Jacobsen—a local volunteer at the Cedar Valley Fire Department. She had met him more than a year ago, the night Leah got engaged.

Adam was a dominant man who knew what he wanted —which included Rachel. She was more than impressed with the fact they had hit it off that night with an immediate connection. In fact, it had been Adam who had approached her in the crowd. She still teased him, to this day, that it had been her big ol' belly that had caught his attention, to which he would always reply, "No, that was just an added bonus."

She had fallen hard for him because of the love he had for Ava. They hadn't rushed into things, because she had just gotten out of a relationship—literally hours before they had met that night.

How she was able to meet such an understanding man was beyond her, but she was more than thankful she had. Adam was everything she had ever sought out in a man. He was kind, patient, and he cared more about others than himself. He was selfless, giving, and made a place in his heart and his life for her and Ava. Not to mention, he was a single father and a great one at that. His love for Tyler went above and beyond her expectations of a father's love.

Lost in thought, she hadn't realized that Ava was no longer babbling along with the characters in the video playing in the backseat. Instead, Ava was sound asleep, her reflection in the rearview mirror was peaceful and relaxed, as her long lashes rested along the top of her rosy red cheeks.

Rachel was more than blessed, and she would continue to count her blessings as often as she could—

starting now with a road to a brighter future for her and her daughter.

TAKING lessons from Adam at a young age, Tyler had insisted that he join his school's football team. He no longer wanted to watch from the bleachers, but instead, be out playing on the field.

Adam had raised him alone since he was a toddler. He had been young and in love with Tyler's mother when she had told him they were expecting. Wanting nothing more than a college degree at the time, Adam had decided to give it up in order to help support his son.

A couple of years after the birth of their son, he had proposed, with the goal to make her his future wife. But all of that changed the night a drunk driver had crossed the center line, swerving into her lane, crashing head on with her car, killing her instantly.

That night, he and Ty were watching Power Rangers, pretending to fight off the imaginary enemy, not realizing that Tyler would be forever without a mother from that night forward.

The accident had prompted his willingness to become a firefighter. His other option had been to become a Paramedic, but it was unlikely he would have the time to complete two years of schooling, so had tossed that idea out the window.

His parents had helped watch Ty over the course of trainings, and within a few months, he had his certification completed and had landed a position at the Cedar Valley Fire Department.

Now, Ty was going on ten and they were doing fine. Through years of memories and pictures, Adam was able to tell Tyler about his mother—hoping he did her justice with the stories of their younger years. The fact that her death had happened when Tyler was so young, and their relationship had been in its early stages, he sometimes wondered if he'd ever be able to move forward with his life, and be able to love another woman like he had loved April.

Meeting Rachel had been his saving grace. She had proved there was indeed love after loss, and he was more than willing to let her in, but they had to take things slowly. She had been pregnant when they met, which hadn't bothered him as much as the remembered thoughts of April he'd had when he introduced himself the night of Liam's engagement.

There had been something about Rachel that had caught his attention that night. He had not cared what her story was the night he introduced himself. He was drawn to her for a reason and that reason hadn't been brushed off as coincidence or fate, but rather was a sign from April telling him it was time to move on.

"Dad, look out," Ty hollered across the yard in time for Adam to see the streak of a football coming right at him. Fast reflexes and a love for football had been on his side; otherwise he would have received a black eye with an unwanted broken nose. "Sorry, Dad."

Tossing the ball back to his son and his friends, Adam smiled and waved it off. "It's all right, son."

Letting go of his thoughts in order to focus on the promise he'd made to his son to play ball with him, he jogged toward their imaginary field. "Let's see what

4

you've got," he taunted as he intercepted and dodged being tackled as he ran the length of their backyard towards the imaginary touchdown line. Slamming the ball against the ground, he raised his arms above his head. "And he scores a touchdown for the old man team and the crowd goes wild."

A fit of laughter echoed across the yard as Ava and Rachel rounded the corner of the house. "I figured this is where you'd be."

Straightening his shirt on the way over to them, he asked, "Did you see my touchdown? This old man still has it in him."

Rachel's smile, along with the offset blue in her eyes, radiated and chased a bad day away. He didn't need anything else to be content with having her in his life. And not forgetting about Ava, he swooped down and swept her off her feet, causing a fit of giggles as her tooth-less grin stared back at him. He shouldn't think of her grin as toothless because she had a few razor-sharp teeth that had bitten his finger the other night, while helping out with the nightly routine of getting ready for bed. Rachel had insisted that Ava use the rubber toothbrush, but since the night Ava had clamped down on his finger, he insisted she rather not.

"I think it's great that you're out here playing with your son and his friends," Rachel said, waving to an excited Tyler as he jogged towards her. "But I wouldn't go as far as saying you're an old man."

"Well, thanks for boosting my ego," he called out. Watching his son wrap his arms around Rachel in the tightest hug possible was a reassuring breath of fresh air. Rachel was more than welcomed here at home, and in

Cedar Valley. Everyone, including Ty, loved her. "Hey, bud, what do you say we start hauling things in from her car?"

Tyler rose from his knees after giving Ava a high-five. "Sure, Dad, can my friends help?"

Shrugging, unsure if they'd actually volunteer to help out an old man who had defeated them, Adam said, "Sure. The more help we have, the sooner we can enjoy the rest of our night."

Turning towards his friends in the backyard, Tyler waved them over. "Come help us."

The young men didn't hesitate much longer than a second when Tyler mentioned playing video games once they were done. A few of the boys were the sons of a couple of buddies at work. Being the same age as his son, or close to it, he had known them since they were born.

Hauling boxes and totes from the car into the house, he had a feeling this was the right move. Tyler had welcomed her openly the night he had met her—shortly after a few months of dating, because he hadn't wanted to introduce Ty to someone who wouldn't be sticking around long, which had been his biggest fear all along.

"Heck, I say they're doing a good enough job, I should take a break," Adam said, hauling the heaviest tote up the stairs, imagining it was full of womanly things like clothes and shoes. He could only imagine Rachel would need a whole closet to herself with her city fashion—a remarkable one at that. He loved the way she dressed up in sundresses and sandals. She could pull off any look—including jogging pants and one of his hoodies, which he loved to see her wear. There was something about a woman wearing his clothes.

"Hey, Dad, this one's the last one," Tyler said, carrying a small box that rattled noisily up the front porch steps—Adam guessed it was full of Ava's toys.

Turning back to Rachel, he pointed his thumb behind him, "See what I mean, they're machines and can handle anything this old man can't."

The dimples in her cheeks were dominantly the first feature he had noticed about her way back when. It was hard to believe they had been dating for over a year now. Ava had been just over two months old when they had officially started dating—making it clear to Rachel's ex, Scott, that she was no longer available for his foolish games. Which, looking back, had only pissed him off, but since then, they hadn't heard from Ava's dad and they saw no problem with that.

"What do you say we order pizza?" he asked the group of young adolescent boys who were now searching through his fridge in an attempt to eat him out of the house. Knowing from experience, and growing up with a brother, he knew exactly what being hungry meant—raiding the fridge every half hour for something to eat. "What kind does everyone like?"

Rachel stepped into the kitchen with Ava on her hip. She laughed at the sight before them. "I'd think they'd eat anything."

"You're probably right," he said, pulling the phone out of his pocket. "Pepperoni? Anchovies?"

The boys pulled their attention from the fridge and gave him a strange look. "Anchovies?" was asked in unison, followed by gagging sounds.

"All right, I'll get that ordered right away," he said,

giving Rachel a side wink as he turned to leave the kitchen.

"No, Dad, wait," Tyler called out, trailing close behind Adam. "Get us pepperoni, please?"

Dialing the number for the pizza place, he nodded. "All right, I'll tell them to add anchovies too."

Teasing Ty and his friends was usually the highlight of his days. Nothing ever failed to make him laugh harder than the bantering between them.

"Come on, Dad, no. You can't be serious."

Finally realizing he hadn't asked Rachel what kind she would like, he turned to her and asked, "Is there a certain kind that you would like?"

"Pepperoni sounds good to me."

She wasn't difficult to please, he liked that about her. The only thing he found that would be difficult was getting used to having a woman in the house. He and April hadn't made it that far in their relationship. The only woman he had ever had in the same house was his mother, before he and Ty had decided it was time to move out on their own.

Ordering the pizza, requesting for delivery instead of carry out, Adam placed his phone on the table in the dining room next to his pager. He had the night off, but he kept it on just in case they needed an extra man.

"It'll be here within the next half hour, so go on and I'll call you back in when it's here."

Shooing the boys back to their football game outside, he closed the door behind them. Ava waddled up to him, stretching her tiny arms around his knee. "Dadda."

Looking to Rachel for confirmation, he pointed down at Ava, "What did she just say?"

"I think you heard her correctly," Rachel said. "She's been hearing Ty call you that a lot lately, so it's her new favorite word."

The fact that Ava wasn't his hadn't stopped him from treating her as his own. To be honest, if things continued to get serious, he planned to adopt Ava someday soon.

———————————————

2

*A*va calling Adam dad was a new thing, so new that it had taken Rachel hearing it a few times to understand exactly what she was saying. Adam had only heard it for the first time tonight and his facial expression, full of shock and love, had overwhelmed her emotions.

Ava calling Adam *daddy* was a sure sign that things were going just the way they wanted them to and they would only continue to get better with each passing day.

She had never loved a man with a child before Adam, so this whole experience was different for her. But when Adam told her the story of Tyler's mother, she realized that this would be more challenging for him than it would be for her.

The thought of Adam loving someone so much, and then losing that person, broke her heart. She couldn't imagine the pain that would have caused in his life. And then to raise the son the two of them had brought into this world...

The ringing of the bell, along with Ava's clapping in excitement, brought her back to the moment. Swooping Ava off her feet, Adam rushed to the door with his wallet.

There was a reason she loved this man, and this moment proved to be that reason. Clapping her hands, she offered her outstretched arms for Ava to come to her, but the little turkey turned away from her, too preoccupied with what Adam had to offer.

Rachel decided to gather the boys from the backyard, since her daughter was content. Pulling the sliding door open, she hollered out to them, who were now in head on tackle mode. "Boys, come get cleaned up. The food's here."

A dead stop followed by a stampede of sweaty boys followed her back to the house. Standing to the side of the door so she wouldn't get run over, she waited for them to make their way around the kitchen. She watched each one, making sure they each washed their hands before grabbing a plate.

"That didn't take long," Adam said, clearing an empty box from the counter. "I'm glad I ordered more than our usual two."

Rachel laughed, reaching for a plate and a couple of slices for her and Ava to share. "I'm thinking you made the right choice."

She watched as his muscles flexed under his shirt as he laughed. Pulling a chair away from the table, she put Ava's highchair in its place. Tearing a slice of pizza into small pieces, she placed a few in front of Ava. She had been trying new foods recently, but they hadn't tried pizza yet. Ava was on a kick of loving mashed potatoes, which was something Rachel hadn't expected, but her mother had warned her that children love mashed potatoes, and loved making a mess with them too.

Ava's face lit up as she chewed through her first piece. Rachel couldn't help but laugh at the expression. "Is that yummy?"

Ava clapped and grabbed another piece from the tray. Rachel took a bite of her own while making sure Ava was able to chew what she had in her mouth, occasionally having to tell her to slow down and take one piece at a time.

It was nearing seven o'clock by the time they had finished supper. The boys were upstairs wrestling around and playing video games for the next hour, while Rachel rocked with Ava in the living room chair. Adam had offered to set the crib up tonight, but Rachel insisted that the playpen would be fine for the night.

A half hour later, Ava was sleeping soundly against Rachel's chest. As much as Rachel enjoyed moments like this, she needed to put Ava down so she could get some things unpacked before it got too late. There would always be tomorrow for whatever couldn't get done tonight.

Kissing Ava on the forehead, Rachel tucked her in under a few light and soft blankets that had become her favorites over the course of the last week or so.

Following Rachel to the den, where they had placed all of her totes and boxes, Adam said, "I'm really happy you and Ava are here."

Sometimes his words caught her off guard, and still being new to this whole mother thing and dealing with emotions and lack of sleep, Rachel's eyes filled with tears. There was nowhere else she'd rather be, than here with him. It had taken them a while to decide on this together, but the time taken had been well worth the wait.

"I love you, Rachel," he whispered, his breath against the back of her neck sent chills through her body, leaving goosebumps trailing behind.

"I love you, too," she said, turning to face him. She wrapped her arms around his neck and allowed him to distract her from the daunting task of unpacking. "You know I should probably unpack so we can enjoy tomorrow without having this waiting for us after the pancake breakfast."

"There's still plenty of time tonight," he said, guiding her out onto the back porch. "Right now, I want to show you something. No peeking."

Following close behind him, with his hand covering her eyes so she couldn't see, she placed one bare foot in front of the other until they walked through the patio doors, and she felt the chilled wood under her feet. "What are you going to show me?"

Ignoring her, the sound of metal scraped against the wood as he slid a chair out, he sat first, and then asked her to sit on his lap. Only when she was relaxed did he remove his hand and allow her to look. Uncertain about what he wanted her to look at; she offered him a puzzled glance.

She should have known, when he pointed up to the sky. Cedar Valley had the biggest sky she had ever seen, and tonight it was full of bright stars that offered the perfect backdrop for the full moon above them.

"It's so beautiful," she whispered, still looking up in awe.

"Much like you," he said, brushing a hand through her

hair as he pushed it aside, revealing her neck for his passionate kisses, which trailed their way from her ear and down to her collar bone. "You're more beautiful than a million stars combined."

3

*F*inally being able to hold her at night had been something he'd looked forward to since the day they officially decided she would be moving in with him. Taking things slowly had seemed to drag time along further, torturing themselves with each passing day, but Adam was sure that it was well worth waiting for.

The morning had come too soon, with the boys hooting and hollering and Ava screaming for breakfast, Adam and Rachel both climbed out of bed, resisting the urge to stay under the covers.

"Breakfast will be in an hour," Adam told Ava, knowing she wouldn't understand a dang word about time. Lifting her up, he put her in the high chair. With Ava screaming and babbling behind him, he reached into the cupboard for the box of Cheerios.

He dumped a handful or two on the tray in front of Ava, who, in exchange for his cereal, offered him a heart-melting smile. There was no doubt he could get used to this.

"Boys!" he hollered from the kitchen doorway at the boys who were now jumping around the living room like a bunch of wild banshees. "Hey! If you have that much energy, take your butts upstairs and get ready. We're leaving in less than thirty minutes."

The annual pancake breakfast began years ago, way before he was born. His father, then a rookie firefighter at the ripe age of twenty-one, had set up the first breakfast event to the public in an attempt to bring in funds for equipment for the department. More than thirty years later it was still going strong.

"There's my little girl," Rachel sang as she walked into the kitchen. Ava extended her arm toward Rachel, pinching a cheerio between her tiny finger and thumb. "For me?" Rachel asked, and Ava giggled as Rachel ate what she had been offered. "Thank you, Miss Ava."

Adam watched the interaction between mother and daughter. Rachel combed a hand through Ava's blonde curls and landed a kiss against the girl's forehead. Ava screeched with excitement, bouncing her arms and legs in unison until Rachel freed her from the highchair.

"Is there time for little miss to get a bath?"

Adam glanced at the clock on the stove. "There's plenty of time."

Ava waved and blew him a kiss as Rachel carried her out of the kitchen in the direction of the downstairs bathroom. Since Rachel was going to be busy giving Ava a bath, he decided to go upstairs to get to work in the spare bedroom.

They had brought the majority of Ava's things last weekend, but he had been swamped with fire calls and hadn't had time to put the crib together. Now was a good time, since the rest of the house was getting ready.

Lining the pieces up in order of their assumed placement, Adam realized it had been more than ten years since he had put a crib together. Without an instruction manual, he hoped this was an easy feat, and they'd end up with something that looked like a crib once he was done.

The pitter patter of tiny feet coming from the hallway told him that Ava was done with her bath. Ava entered her new room first, Rachel coming in close second.

Adam hadn't noticed that time had gotten away from him. The boys had taken off outside for another round of football while he finished putting the last railing up. "I figured I'd get this done while waiting," he said, rubbing a stiff kink out of his neck. "I didn't have instructions, and the last time I put a crib together was before Tyler was even born, so it took me a lot longer than I had imagined it would."

He had placed it in the corner of the room, opposite side of the window. He wasn't Martha Stewart or any other homemaker or designer, but he wanted Ava to have the best room a little girl could dream of. He had positioned her things strategically around the room, leaving enough room for play. He also wanted Ava to be able to wake up to the beautiful view of the mountains, so he had left her window clutter-free.

"It's beautiful," Rachel said, in awe of the room and what he had done with it. "What do you think Ava? Do you like your new room?"

Ava clapped and the few teeth she did have made an appearance in her goofy cheeky grin, which he enjoyed seeing. Ava squirmed, wanting down from her mother's hold, and after Rachel complied with her wishes, she walked over to her wooden toy box and pulled toys out, tossing them next to her feet.

Adam watched as Rachel squatted next to her and asked her to pick only one toy so they could get going. As though Ava understand every word her mother had said, she picked up a baby and held it out for her mother to grab. "Are you sure this is the one you want to take? Ok, then," Rachel said, turning back to Adam, "I think we're ready to go."

Clapping his hands, he turned toward the hallway and led them down the stairs. He would gather the boys from the backyard, and they would be on their way.

THE FIRE DEPARTMENT sat angled on a corner lot, centered perfectly with a flag pole and a painted rock next to it. Cars lined the curbs bumper to bumper as they pulled up. Adam hadn't been joking when he said it was one of the most anticipated events of the year here in Cedar Valley—something that everyone looked forward to, which was evident by the number of cars.

Unbuckling Ava from her car seat, Rachel was more than excited to get inside. It was almost like a family reunion. Being able to see people she hadn't seen for a while. Tyler and his buddies jumped out of the back of the truck and ran toward the building.

"Hey, make sure you remember your manners!" Adam hollered after them, smiling at Rachel as he made his way around the front of the truck. Wrapping an arm around her, he pulled her close as they walked toward the entrance. Adam held the door open as she and Ava walked in.

The place was packed, and several familiar faces turned in the direction of the door as it opened. Excitement thrummed the area as smiles and friendly waves were offered as they walked in. Adam had told her they were all family here, and he hadn't been kidding.

"Rachel, I'm so glad you could make it," Adam's mother said, above the noise of the crowd as she closed the distance between them. She reached for Ava, and without hesitation, Ava went into her arms. "Come to gramma. How about we get Ava a pancake?"

Rachel smiled, allowing Adam's mother to take Ava toward the kitchen. Rachel had loved his parents since the day she had met them. She had actually met them at Leah's wedding, before Adam and she were an official couple.

"Rachel!"

Turning in the direction of the voice that had called out to her, she saw Leah running up to her, or at least doing her best to run—it was more of a waddled attempt than anything. She had informed Rachel of the good news after several pregnancy tests read positive. And when she said several, she meant several, more than ten. She remembered Leah telling her that she had taken so many because she wanted to be sure—leaving no room for error.

Stretching out her arms to prepare for Leah's hug, Rachel waited, hiding a laugh because she remembered all too well the days of being too pregnant to hurry. "It feels like I haven't seen you in forever."

It had only been a month. They hadn't seen each other, but their nightly phone calls had become a routine that both Liam and Adam had grown accustomed to—like they really had a choice in the matter.

"Leah, you look amazing," Rachel said. She wasn't lying either. Leah pulled off the pregnancy look. She was cuter than heck with a baby bump. "I'm so jealous because I looked like a hot air balloon with Ava."

"Not at all," Leah argued. "I look like a Goodyear blimp."

Laughing, Leah nearly peed her pants. No matter what Leah truly thought of herself, Rachel would be there to defend her against harsh thoughts. They were the best of friends, always there for each other, and they always would be, no matter what.

"Have you two decided on a name yet?"

"Hold that thought," Leah said, holding a finger up before darting off toward the restrooms.

Flagging Rachel over, Adam stood in line next to Liam and Conner. Conner had joined the Jacobsen family tradition of joining the fire department in his early twenties. The first time she had met Conner, she hadn't needed anyone to tell her he and Adam were brothers. With the Jacobsen resemblance, there was no mistaking any of them for relation.

Adam reached for her hand and squeezed her in next to him in line. Making their way into the kitchen, following the line that led them around the u-shaped counter, Rosie called out to her from behind the mixer. "Rachel! It's good to see you!"

"You too, Rosie!"

Rosie was looking better and better every day. After having her stroke and scaring everyone, Rosie had pulled through and made a full recovery. Leah had told her all about the love story between Wes and Rosie, which only made her think of her own grandparents who'd passed away years ago. She had always looked up to her grandparents, and other elderly couples who represented what true love really was.

Wes and Rosie were definitely the prime example of such love. They had been through a lot together and still, they were by each other, never once faltering or leaving the other one's side.

"You'll have to come visit sometime soon," Rosie said, offering Rachel a hot pancake right off the griddle. "I help out at the coffee shop during the week and sometimes on Saturday mornings, if you're ever in the area early in the morning."

Rachel would have to take her up on the offer, because starting next week, she had her first day at the local elementary. "Sounds good. I'll see you soon."

Making her way through the kitchen, she found Adam's mother and Ava chatting at a table nearby. Rachel sat down across from them, leaving a seat for Adam to sit next to her. She offered to take Ava, but his mother insisted she was just fine.

Conner sat across from them, next to his mother and Ava. It didn't take him long to scarf down his food and hold his arms out for Ava to come see him. She hesitated for a minute, but soon enough, she was reaching past Nana for him to grab her. "Come see Uncle Conner."

The love this family had for her and Ava had been felt

since the day Adam welcomed them into his life. His family had become her family, and she loved them all the same. She was more than blessed to have them in her and Ava's life.

4

*L*ike every year before, the pancake breakfast was a hit. People from surrounding towns, including many of their local supporters, crowded the fire department with their families. The pancakes tasted excellent, a huge thanks, once again, to Rosie and her cooking.

It had been a great turn out, raising more than a thousand dollars for the department. Cedar Valley loved their firefighters, and were willing to donate more money and time if needed—more than half the town had said so, and today proved it.

"I'm going to finish cleaning up here, if you want to take the kids home?" Saying the word kids and home in the same sentence had a good feel to it. Handing Rachel the keys to his truck, she accepted and smiled. He'd do whatever it took to keep her smiling like that. "Hey, actually, Ty, why don't you stay here and help out?"

He and Ty had a great relationship—stronger than any

other ordinary father and son bond—stronger than his with his own father. Some of that was because of everything they had been through, but most of it was because he had vowed to be the best father he could be, and at the same time, he'd promised to instill good values and bring his son up right, just like his grandfather and father had done with him and his brother. Cedar Valley made it easy, because in this town, there was a sense of knowing what is right, and there wasn't one person who was afraid to set someone on the straight and narrow path.

With not much fuss, Ty agreed to stay behind as he waved to Rachel and Ava. Rachel had offered to stay and help, but Ava needed a nap and he was sure she would become fussy if she didn't get one.

"Are you going to need us to come back and pick you up?" Rachel asked, holding tight to a squirming Ava.

"Nope, I'm sure we'll be able to find someone to give us a ride back to the farm."

Rachel smiled, switched Ava to her other hip, leaned in to him for a quick kiss. "I love you."

He kissed Ava. The girl had his heart. It hadn't taken long for that to happen, a few weeks after Rachel and he had started dating, the baby had him wrapped around her tiny finger.

A group hug happened between Tyler, Rachel and Ava, and if Adam hadn't already known he was in love with this little family of his, he'd be sure of it now.

"We'll see you after a while, be careful driving home," he called out, as Rachel and Ava walked away. Turning around, he jogged up behind Tyler. "Hey, you're not upset that I asked you to stay and help, are you?"

Tyler shrugged. "Not really."

The nonchalant way Tyler responded, with his slumped shoulders, flagged Adam's attention. It hadn't been like Tyler to act down and out. He was always upbeat and cheerful—like an average ten year old boy was supposed to be.

"Hey bud, is there something you need to talk about?" Adam asked, reaching out to grab hold of his son's arm. Standing by the big, old oak tree, he offered a listening ear to his son. "Whatever is bothering you, you can tell me."

It was written all over his son's face. There was something that was bothering him, something had come over him within the last few minutes and he wanted to make sure he was okay. Whatever it was, he would try his best to understand.

"Dad, do you think Rachel and Ava will stay with us forever?"

Confusion hit him like a flat hand across the face. For a ten year old to have to wonder this... it broke his heart. How was he to explain that Rachel and Ava would be with them forever when the boy had lost his mother? There was no forever, there was only today, because tomorrow was never promised. He hated the fact that life wasn't all about forevers and sweet things. Life was real, and in real life, unexpected things happened every day. Things that a ten year old shouldn't have to worry about, but here was his son, matured by the death of his mother, but still a boy with a heavy heart.

"Son, as much as I would like to say it, I can't." His throat was closing as the emotion he was trying to handle choked him. He wasn't afraid of showing his son emotions, because grown men did cry, regardless of what one wanted to believe. He had cried for days, and still cried to this day after losing April. There was no shame in crying. "I'm sure they'll stick around for as long as they're able to. By the grace of God, we'll be a family for however long we're on this earth."

Tyler nodded, showing a fair understanding of what Adam was trying to tell him. It had been difficult, over the years, to depend on his faith to guide them through this tragedy, especially when the first thing a person wanted to do was blame the power above them for allowing such an awful thing to happen. In order to provide a patient understanding with Tyler, he'd had to free himself of all negativity and lean on his faith to carry him through the last ten years of his life, and he was now more than thankful for having a higher power to believe in.

"Let's get things done here so we can go home," Adam said, patting his son on the shoulder. "I'll race ya to it."

Giving his son a two second lead over him, he watched Tyler sprint ahead before taking off after him.

Out of breath and bending over, Adam stopped short of the open bay doors. Tyler was a helluva runner. He needed to get in better shape if he was going to keep up with him.

"Nice try, Dad," Tyler teased, patting him on the shoulder. "An A for your effort."

"What happened? You beat your old man?" Liam asked, coming around the corner of the building. Liam didn't hesitate to slap Adam on the back. "Getting too old to be running like that, Champ."

"Look who's talkin'!" Adam hollered after him.

Liam turned before getting into his truck. Offering up a mocking smirk, he said, "I'm not the one racing against a kid. I know better."

"Yeah, whatever," Adam said, waving him off. There was a good chance that he should probably get back to running every morning. It had been a while since he had last seen the sun rise over the mountains in Cedar Valley.

Folding tables and carrying them upstairs to the loft above the station, Adam thought about getting back to his morning runs. He was sure that Tyler would enjoy it, and Rachel wouldn't mind.

"What are you thinking about, old man?"

Coming down the stairs to find Liam and his brother Conner at the landing looking up, he said, "Nothing, why?"

"I think you're thinking about getting home to the hottie that's waiting for you," Conner said, wiggling his eyebrows, looking like an idiot.

Giving his arm a brotherly shove, Adam said, "That's not how you should talk about women. Someday you'll understand."

Liam laughed. "Someday will never come for him. That's wishful thinking there."

"Shut it," Conner said, sticking out his bottom lip. The kid still had growing up to do. Being in his twenties didn't mean anything when it came to maturity. Boys didn't mature until their late twenties, early thirties. Adam would pray for the woman who got stuck with Conner.

Rounding up the last of the chairs, Adam called out for Tyler to follow him out. There was nothing left to do, everyone had cleaned up the place and it looked good.

"We'll see ya this weekend, won't we?" Adam's mother asked, hugging them. "I didn't get a chance to say bye to Rachel and Ava. I hope they come with you guys this weekend."

"We'll be there, Mom," Adam said, wondering how he could have forgotten their plans of going to his parent's house. Sunday dinners were a weekly necessity in his family—a tradition he hoped to continue on with his own kids. "I'm sure Rachel would love to come."

5

A loud rumble was heard coming down the gravel road, and it slowed near the driveway. Rachel opened the front door and watched as Liam's truck came to a sudden stop, allowing Adam and Tyler to jump out. Leah sat in the front seat, with her hand waving out the window in Rachel's direction.

Rachel walked out onto the front porch, trying not to be too loud because Ava was still sleeping. "Hey, Lee!"

"We'd stay and visit, but I need to go home and take a nap," Leah said. "I'll call you later or tomorrow, though."

Waving until they took off down the road, Rachel stood on the porch long after Tyler had gone inside. "I've missed that girl."

Leaning into his kiss, she smiled. It was good to finally have a place where she belonged. She felt it deep within her heart. She finally had what Leah had told her about. "Well, I missed you," he said, pressing his lips against hers, she could smell the scent of his cologne—a mix she wouldn't get tired of.

"It's only been a couple of hours," she said, playing with the button on his shirt.

"Two hours too long," he replied, kissing her with passion as he pushed her up against the railing.

Laughing, she gently pushed him back. "Get out of here and find something else to do."

"Rejected once again," he pouted, walking up the rest of the stairs to the porch. "I see how it is."

"I haven't rejected you once," Rachel said, trailing behind him. "Do you even know what rejection is?"

Turning, his eyes met hers, and in that moment she saw the desire that yearned for her attention. In that same exact moment, if there hadn't been any kids in the house, she would have allowed him to have his way with her. Cursing those eyes of his, along with his sweet charm, she followed him into the house.

"Do you want to help me bake some cookies?" she asked Tyler, who was antsy and looking for something to do.

"Only if we make my favorite kind."

It hadn't taken her long to figure out that Ty loved baking as much as he loved playing football. The last weekend she had spent with him and Adam, she had prepared supper for them and had settled in the kitchen to bake their dessert. It hadn't taken long before Ty was in there with her, asking if he could help out. In spite of all of the gender roles society places on kids, she had seen nothing wrong with a boy learning how to cook or bake.

"Hmm... I can't remember what your favorite is," she teased, tousling his hair with a playful hand. His hair was light brown, with natural highlights from the bright and warm summer sun. She adored his eyes, the color of a warm sky, much like his father's.

"Chocolate chip! How can you not remember?" Tyler asked, sliding into position near the mixer on the counter.

"The question is... how could I ever forget?" She smiled at his puzzled expression as he tried to figure out whether she had forgotten or not. "What do you say we bake extra for church on Sunday?"

She had never been a church goer, but Adam's faith had guided her in a new direction. Meeting Adam and Ty, moving to Cedar Valley, going to church on Sundays—it was all a new beginning for her, and she was enjoying every minute of it.

"How many dozens will we have to make?"

Chuckling at the s he added to dozen, she said, "I'm thinking we'll make two double batches."

She watched as he tried counting the number of cookies that would be on his fingers. He was a math whiz in school, according to his grades—all A's and B's—which had earned him a few dollars from his father.

"If you're trying to figure out how many cookies that will be, let's take a look at how many the recipe says one batch will provide," she offered, pulling the recipe card from the box and handing it to him. "Can you find where it says how many one batch offers?"

"Twenty-four?" Tyler said, raising an eyebrow in disbelief.

"Sounds about right," she said, tying an apron around her waist when she felt two steady hands take hold of the strings for her.

"I'm going to run to Levy's for a bit," Adam said, tying her apron as he snuck in a few kisses on the back of her neck. "Since it looks like you've got everything under control here."

"Of course," she said, leaning into his hold as his warm lips pressed against the side of her neck, sending goosebumps along her skin.

Tyler scrunched his face and made gagging noises. "Get a room!"

Adam tousled his son's hair before grabbing him in for a one arm hug as he planted a kiss on the top of his head. Rachel knew one day soon, Tyler would be too grown for his father to kiss him and love on him. "I'll see you two after a while. Don't have too much fun while I'm gone," Adam said, offering a quick wave and a wink before he headed out the back door. Peeking his head back into the kitchen, he said, "And save me some."

Rachel watched out the window as he climbed into his truck and headed for the end of the drive. Levy's had picked up plenty of business since it had been rebuilt after the fire. It had become the main spot in town for gatherings and parties. Everyone loved Liam and Leah, and they most certainly loved Levy's just as much.

Allowing Tyler to pour the ingredients into the mixing bowl, she prepared the cookie sheets and preheated the oven. She had to help him with the measurements, but other than that, he was doing fine by himself. "Keep that up, you're going to make a woman happy someday," she teased, pulling oven mitts from the drawer next to him as she nudged him.

His scrunched nose and overly dramatic reaction to her teasing had made it fun for her. Adam had told her that he was at the stage of being curious about other girls, crushing on them, but at the same time thinking they all had cooties.

She recalled her childhood of having cooties and the whole "circle circle dot dot, now I have my cootie shot" anthem that they had sung out loud at recess every day any time a boy had tried to touch them.

"I think I want to be a baker when I grow up," Tyler said, breaking the silence with these surprising words.

"Really?" Rachel asked, unsure of how to direct this conversation. Wiping her hands on her apron, she pulled out a couple of eggs for him to crack; she decided to just see where the conversation would journey off to.

"Yeah," Tyler shrugged, and Rachel could see the hesitation furrow his eyebrows. "I know that most boys don't bake or even cook, but one day I'd like to own a bakery and offer the best pancakes in town."

The boy had quite the imagination. She was certainly impressed that being only ten, he was coming up with ideas for his future. Whether or not they would endure and actually happen, she knew that was yet too far away to see.

"First off, there are plenty of men who bake and cook," Rachel said, locking the mixer in place before allowing him to hit the power. "And second of all, you'd better decide on another tasty treat, because I'm sure your dad wouldn't like you competing against the fire department's pancakes."

Laughing, he hit the power and watched the mixer beat the dough. Rachel stood at the ready with a spatula in hand. She was proud of this moment with Tyler, even more so that he wanted to go out on a limb and do something that wasn't the society's norm for a boy to do. Football and baking—a cheerleader might fall for that.

Shutting the mixer down, she went to stir the dough. "Um, Ty, guess what we forgot."

Peeking over the side of the bowl, Tyler looked up at her and stifled a laugh with his hand. "The chocolate chips!"

Their laughter echoed throughout the kitchen as she reached into the cupboard for the container of chocolate chips. "What's a chocolate chip cookie without the chocolate chips?"

"Chipless?" Tyler answered, with a grin that was missing a few teeth.

Surprised that he had answered a question she hadn't thought had an answer, she couldn't help but laugh harder as she handed him the container of their missing chocolate. "You might want to think about becoming a comedian, too, while you're at it."

Ava's cry sounded over the baby monitor sitting across from them on the table. Grabbing it, she looked back at Tyler, "Think you can manage without me for a few minutes, Baker Tyler?"

His smile—full of charm and confidence—told her he would be able to handle anything, much like his father.

6

"Do you think she'll say yes?" he asked, opening the small black box in his hand, as he showed it off to the guys surrounding the counter.

The guys had planned to meet up here at Levy's today to shoot the shit. Wes and Edward were at the end of the counter, shooting back their own concoction. His grandfather and Wes had become good friends back in 1976, or so they say, when Cedar Valley had become Cedar Valley. Adam could recite their story word for word, from all the times he'd had to hear it.

"That's the million dollar question, man," Liam said, popping the top of his beer. "Do you think she'll say yes?"

If Adam had to bet everything he owned, he would like to venture the answer would be yes. More so, he would love for her to say yes. Buying a ring and preparing for this moment had taken him years, and he wasn't sure how he'd react to an answer different than yes.

"She'd better," Adam said, laughing as he threw back the last swallow of his beer.

Setting down the empty bottle, which was soon collected by Megan, Rosie's granddaughter and one of the best paramedics Cedar Valley had, Adam thanked her and requested another.

"You know what they say," Liam said, nudging Adam in the arm. "Wait too long, the answer will be no."

Megan brought his beer back to him. "Sorry to interrupt whatever you two are talking about, but do you know when Conner will be back in town?"

Conner had ventured back this way from northern Colorado this weekend in time for the pancake breakfast, but had left no sooner than he arrived. "I'm not sure," Adam said, taking a long drink from the bottle. He had always had his suspicion that there was something between those two—Megan and Conner. In his opinion, Conner was still too young to understand a woman, let alone treat her right. He was focused on making enough money to booze it up on the weekends—the only time made for women was in between the sheets at parties. Adam wasn't going to tell Megan that. She was smart enough to know.

As if she realized she might have offered too much of something going on, she said, "I only ask because he mentioned he might be moving back."

"That's news to me," Adam said, twisting the lid off his beer. He would only have a couple before venturing back home. This weekend was his only weekend off call, and it had been a while since he'd had a few drinks. "What's his plan when he gets back here?"

Megan shrugged, and he watched her walk back to the other end of the counter. Turning to Liam, he asked, "Have you heard anything about that?"

Liam held his hands up in defense. "Nope, not a single thing."

He and Conner were almost a decade apart in age. Conner had been a 'whoops' made by their parents, but had been welcomed regardless. Adam had made a promise to protect him throughout the years of growing up, which he had kept. They weren't as close now as they had been, but that was only because Conner had decided to move to Colorado to fight fires instead of sticking around Cedar Valley. It was always like his brother to want something bigger and better, more exciting, and that's what he got out in Colorado—the same view of the mountains and fresh air, but more fires to fight.

"Hey, man, don't think too much on what she said," Liam said, nudging Adam back to reality. "You know how guys are. Conner was probably just fluffing her pillow."

"Yeah," Adam said, tipping back the bottle and gulping the last of his beer. The thought of Conner coming home to stay would be on his mind from now until the day he decided to actually go through with it.

"Besides, you have bigger things to figure out and plan for," Liam offered, slapping him on the back. "Like, how you're going to get Rachel to say yes."

He wasn't as worried about Rachel saying no, as he was his brother moving back to Cedar Valley. Their father had retired from the department more than six months ago, and though Conner had denied it to be the reason he had moved to Colorado, Adam knew their father had been the reason Conner hadn't signed on with their department. Conner had a rough bond with their father, and Adam could bet their father's retirement had been the invite back to Cedar Valley that Conner had been waiting for.

our batches of cookies later, two naps for Ava, and a football game on television, Rachel was now sitting with her little family in the living room, waiting for Adam to come home.

It hadn't bothered her that he had gone into town, because she knew this was his only weekend off this month. Lately, the shifts had been left open and needed to be filled, leaving Adam no choice but to take call. She knew he enjoyed it, otherwise he wouldn't do it, but she prayed that they would find more volunteers so the ones they had wouldn't get burned out.

The sound of gravel crunching alerted them to Adam's arrival home. She couldn't wait for him to walk into the house as she hurried out onto the back porch to greet him with a quick hug and kiss. She was determined to get used to this, and he made it so easy.

Turning her head to the side as he buried his nose into her collar bone, she said, "I've missed you."

"Mmm, I can smell those cookies on you," he said,

pressing firm kisses along her neck. "You smell so sweet, I could almost eat you."

Laughter escaped as he spun her around and gave her a love tap. The kids waited by the back door as he walked in. Ava raised her arms in the air, screeching for him to pick her up. He swooped down and cradled her against his chest. With a free arm, he squeezed Tyler into his side. "Hey Bud, how'd baking go?"

Adam was the type of father every woman dreamed of having for their kids. He was hands on, active in their lives, never missing a single minute of asking them about their lives. Even with a thousand things on his plate, he refused to let them down.

"I think Tyler has something he would like to share with you," Rachel said, glancing at Tyler in an attempt to encourage him.

Tyler looked up at Adam and back to Rachel. "I love baking, Dad. Rachel and I made a lot of cookies."

Expecting nothing less from Adam, Rachel waited for his reaction when Tyler told him that he wanted to be a baker. "Owning your own bakery?"

"Yeah!" Tyler said, pumping a fist into the air. "I could make the best pancakes in town."

Adam's eyes widened with surprise as he looked between Rachel and Tyler. Pointing a finger in Tyler's direction, he asked, "Did he just say the best pancakes?"

Rachel nodded, her smile couldn't get any bigger than it was already. His love for Tyler screamed for all women to swoon. The way he interacted with the children, causing them laughter beyond tears and excitement, caused her heart to beat fast at the thoughts of finally finding the right place, the right man, and the right kind of life.

"Well, I'll probably need Rachel's help," Tyler said, his smile melted Rachel's heart.

"No way, she's mine. You can't have her," Adam teased, passing a wink her way. "Are you sure you want to compete with the pancake breakfast?"

Adam sounded a little worried, but it was all in good fun. Tyler nodded his head. "Yes, I could make a lot of money on them every day and donate it, Dad."

Rachel could feel her heart turn to mush as she watched the interaction between the father and son. Adam still had a strong hold on Ava, not letting her out of his arms before he brought out the tickle monster. Ava screamed in panic as she raced toward Rachel in the doorway. She clung tight to Rachel's leg, begging for her mother to lift her up. When Rachel didn't lift her, Ava let go and ran for the living room, tripping over the rug on her way in. Adam followed close behind her and once she had fallen, the rest was history.

Ava's laughter echoed off the walls, bouncing with slight shrills of shrieks as Adam brought the tickle monster under her chin and it trailed to her underarms.

Tyler's laugh caused Rachel to turn around, her eyes wide, her smile bigger, as he shook his head and turned to run away. He quickly dodged her as he ducked under her arm and ran for the stairs, spinning full circle to see where she was, he missed his step and slid across the hardwood floor of the living room. Diverting to plan b he took off through the living room toward the dining area that would lead him back to the kitchen.

She had to give him props for being quick on his feet,

as she watched her own footing, making sure she didn't land on her butt in an attempt to get him.

"Go mommy, go!" Ava cheered in between tickles. "Mommy!"

Rachel laughed, continuing her chase as Ava waved at her. Taking a detour, she decided to hide out in the hallway until Tyler made his appearance around the corner. She heard the padding of his socked feet against the hardwood floor and prepared for her attack.

As soon as he came into view, she leapt toward him, tackling him to the floor with laughter and tickling. The surprise on his face as she tackled him had been priceless. The fact that he hadn't seen her coming was even better.

He may have been quick on his feet, but she was quick on her tackling moves and was sure they would only get better with time. Tyler's laughter ricocheted against the floor as he squirmed underneath her hold. He was too old for the tickle monster, but he was still young enough to have fun right along with them.

"Run Tyler, I've got her," Adam hollered from behind her as his strong arms found their way around her as he lifted her away from her captive hold on Tyler. "Go, Tyler, run for your life!"

There was no sense in struggling against his hold, she wouldn't win. Instead she sat back on her heels, causing him to think she was done with the torture. As soon as he relaxed his hold, she darted off in the direction Tyler had escaped. It wasn't over yet. The fun had just gotten started.

8

---

*H*er love for his son was evident in the way she offered to help Tyler with homework, volunteered to give him a ride to school on her way to work, and most definitely, the way she was willing to accept him as her own.

He could say the same for himself with Ava. That little girl with her small blonde, perfectly twisted curls, along with her bright blue eyes and gap-toothed smile, had him wrapped around her finger since day one of meeting her.

He had been with Rachel through the last few months of the pregnancy. He had ventured into the Lamaze classes, not even realizing he had long since decided that he was in their lives and nothing was going to change that.

Meeting Rachel, and later on, Ava, had allowed him to move on from the hurt in his past. Allowed him to love again, and to realize that good things can happen after the bad.

Swiping an arm around her waist, he pulled her in

close. Out of breath, he inhaled as her sweet scent of lilies and lavender infiltrated his senses. He could stay like this for the rest of the night. She made loving her easy, with her long blonde hair and laid back personality, but there were times when her spunkiness shined through along with her stubbornness.

Her head fell back when his lips pressed gently against her neck. Struggling against his arms left him with no choice but pull her in tighter, strengthening his hold on her as he whispered in her ear, "Let's order some pizza... then, what do you say we call it an early night?" Her smile pressed against his cheek and he knew he'd gotten her thinking. "I've been thinking about those cookies all damned day."

A playful slap against his arm, followed by the blush on her cheeks told him that he'd gotten her thinking about other things. Releasing her from his hold, she spun away, giving him a playful warning look. He couldn't wait 'til later.

Sending a wink her way just to watch her squirm with laughter was the highlight of his night, along with chasing his kids around the house.

Assisting Rachel with tackling Tyler had been the ultimate play of the night. Tyler hadn't expected her to come for him again. He had taken a break to grab a glass of water, but no sooner than he returned to the living room than he was tackled and tickled by them both.

The ringing of the doorbell interrupted their fun. "Saved by the bell," he hollered over his shoulder on the way to the door, giving Tyler a shit eating grin, knowing this wasn't over just yet.

Pulling his wallet out of his back pocket, he heard

Rachel corralling the kids to wash their hands and get ready for supper. Opening the door, he was greeted by the delivery boy—who was no older than sixteen and belonged to his longtime friend and county sheriff, Jeff. "Hey, bud, keeping busy tonight?"

The kid shrugged a shy shoulder, offering the two large boxes of pizza with an outstretched hand. He remembered Jeff wanting to get the kid into football, but he hadn't been interested. The boy would have made a heck of a quarterback with those broad shoulders of his.

Swapping the boy a twenty, with a five dollar tip, for the pizza, Adam patted him on the back. "Take it easy, kid. Have a good night."

"You too, sir," the boy said, walking off the porch in the direction of his old beat up Chevy S10.

Hooking the door with his leg, he shut it and made his way to the dining room where Rachel had the kids seated and ready to eat.

"Who's ready to chow down?" Smiling, he placed the pizzas in the middle of the table and couldn't help hearing Ava's sweet voice carry over the chatter as she pleaded for pizza with outstretched arms.

It was only their second night together as a family, but someone who didn't know any better would have guessed longer than that.

9

*I*t didn't make sense that she would be receiving this letter in the mail after all this time. Two years and counting had been long enough for her to believe that he had not wanted anything to do with little Ava.

Tears streamed down her face as she climbed into her car. She hated to know what this letter meant for her and Ava. For all of them. This family she had dreamed of would soon be broken and she couldn't do anything about it.

Unfolding the paper, Rachel reread it, hoping she was mistaken by what it was saying. There was no way that Scott wanted full custody of Ava. Not after being out of her life for the last two years. Hell, he had even moved out of state. What the hell was he thinking?

Folding the paper along its creases, she shoved it back into the plain white envelope she'd dreaded receiving since the day Scott had walked out of their lives, always knowing that one day he could possibly change his mind.

She was no expert in the law, but she knew there was a good chance he could win. It scared her to think of what would happen if he did persuade the court system that he was a good father and that she was a horrible mother, unfit would be the term he would use. He had thrown that word at her a few times the night he had left her.

Shifting the car into drive, she swiped tears from her cheeks and pulled out of the post office parking lot. Steering the car to the right, she headed in the direction of the fire station. Adam was on duty for the next twelve hours and she couldn't wait that long to talk to him. Tyler was at the afterschool program for athletes and Ava would be at the daycare until Rachel picked her up. She had already called to let them know she would be arriving a bit later than usual.

Pulling into an empty spot out of the way of the bay doors, she parked the car and climbed out. Adam and a few of the guys were spraying down their ladder truck when she walked over to him.

"Hey, babe, what's up?"

She couldn't hold back the tears or the quiver in her chin as she rushed into his arms. Burying her face into his chest, he wrapped his arms around her and held onto her. "What's going on?"

Holding the envelope out for him to pull the letter out himself, she waited, while tears streaked down her face, staining mascara against her cheeks.

"What's this?" Adam asked, pointing to the letter before unfolding it. She couldn't say anything other than a mumble of the name that just shattered her life. "Scott?"

She could barely hold herself up. The small piece of creased paper had caused her stomach to flop and her whole world to follow suit. She had no idea what she was going to do. There were quite a few lawyers back home in the city, but she wasn't sure how she would be able to afford one.

"Don't worry about this," Adam said, holding the paper with a tight grip in front of her as he pulled her close and kissed her forehead.

"I'm scared."

Admitting her emotions to Adam had always been easy. He was the comfort she had always needed, and the guidance he offered was priceless, and valued more than words could express.

He didn't need to say anything for her to know that he was just as concerned as she was. This was something new for the both of them.

"If I have a choice in the matter, Scott won't see her, let alone have any kind of visitation rights."

Although his words were meant to comfort her, she didn't find comfort. Instead, she felt a rush of panic and devastation. She knew, deep down, there was no way a court system would keep a child from their father. And there was no way she would be able to prove Scott to be a horrible father by mentioning he hasn't seen her in almost two years.

"I'll give my buddy a call later, or tomorrow, and see what he can do for us," Adam said, kissing her once again on the forehead before pulling her in close as he wrapped his arms around her. "Don't worry too much until we figure out what's going on, okay?"

Pulling herself together had always been easier when the situation didn't involve Ava. So many times, she'd worried about and dreaded this moment. Not because

Scott would be a terrible father, at least she certainly hoped not, but because it had been so long without him in the picture and things were going just fine without him.

"Okay?" he asked, lifting her chin so he could look into her eyes. "My buddy is one of the best lawyers around. I'm sure he'll be able to help us figure it all out."

Nodding, she silently agreed not to worry, knowing all too well that it would be easier said than done. For now, she needed to pick up Ava and keep her mind off of it—not just for her, but for Ava's sake, too.

aking his focus back to his duties as a fireman, he walked back to the rig he had been busy washing with his crew when Rachel pulled up.

The thought of Scott wanting any type of custody of Ava was mind boggling. The jerk hadn't wanted anything to do with her since the day he walked away from Rachel. He would be damned if that guy had anything to do with Ava, not since he was as attached to her as one of his own.

Raising a hand to let the guys know he'd be back over there in a minute, he dug his phone from his pocket. He hadn't talked to Lux for a while—more than a few months now, since he'd picked up extra hours at the station. They used to shoot pool on Friday nights at Levy's when they weren't busy with work and family obligations.

The last time he had talked to Lux was the day the Cedar Valley Fire Department was facing a lawsuit from a bogus claim that had come from the town's crazy lady, who had sworn her cat died in the controlled fire they had a while back. An old, abandoned house that sat next to hers. The case lasted less than a week. Lux had claimed it to be an "open and shut" case.

"Hey, it's been a while. What's up?" Lux answered on the second ring—Adam guessed Lux let it ring long enough for caller id to tell him who was calling.

"Not much, man," Adam said, feeling a bit guilty for not keeping up with his buds. He'd have to plan a night for all of them to get together at Levy's, like old times. "I have a favor to ask you for, though."

A deep chuckle echoed through the phone before Lux said, "Not another crazy woman, I hope?"

"No, thank God; we haven't had any complaints that I know of since then," Adam said, knowing that the department rarely received a complaint worth making note of. "It's about Rachel and Ava."

"I heard they moved into your house," Lux said, taking a minute before asking, "How's she liking Cedar Valley?"

"As far as I know, she loves it."

It hadn't taken long for the news to travel of Rachel and Ava's arrival. He figured as much, especially in this small town. Rachel and Ava hadn't been in the house more than a week, and almost everyone was well aware.

"That's good, I thought she would. How's Tyler doing with everything?"

The fact that Tyler had talked with him the other night about his mother, let Adam know that Tyler was going to be okay with Rachel and Ava. They'd had plenty of conversations over the last year or so, since Rachel and he started dating, and he knew his son would be okay with the transition to a bigger family.

"He's enjoying it. Actually, better than I thought he would be," Adam admitted. He'd had some doubts that

Tyler wouldn't adjust to Rachel, but that doubt went out the window the day Tyler had met her. It was weird, but Adam knew at that moment that everything would be okay. "They baked all day yesterday."

"Baked?" The question was followed by a stifled laugh, but when Lux realized Adam wasn't joking, he cleared his throat and said, "I take it Tyler likes to bake then?"

"Seems to be the case," Adam said, without shame that his son was into baking. "Football and baking. I guess it'll be good for him."

"So, what's this favor that you need from me?"

"Rachel received a letter in the mail stating Scott wants custody of Ava. I told her not to worry, that I'd talk to you and figure out what's going on."

"Has he been in Ava's life at all?"

"Not a single minute." Adam had told Lux about Scott the night they got together at Levy's to bullshit over the whole cat lady incident. "Rachel says he hasn't even asked about Ava, let alone made an attempt to see her."

"I'm not sure he'll get custody, but he will most likely get visitation rights," Lux said, setting it straight from the get-go. "No state will keep a father from their child, at least unless it's necessary."

Adam didn't like the sound of that, but at least he knew there would be a chance that Scott would be in Ava's life—whether Rachel and he liked it or not.

"I'll do a little digging and see what I come up with," Lux said, ending the call with a promise to get back to Adam soon.

Shoving his phone back into the side pocket of his tactical pants, he walked back over to the trucks. He wanted nothing but the best for Rachel and Ava, including a house to call their own, along with whatever else he had to do to make sure they were taken care of.

"Hey, man," One of the newest members of their department hollered out to him. Adam gave a quick wave and kept walking in the direction of the truck. The rookie jogged up behind him and was soon matching him step for step. "I heard your brother might be coming back to Cedar Valley."

The last thing Adam wanted to talk about was his brother. His brother had a lot of making up to do around these parts, which would include mending relations with his father. He loved Conner, but it was clear that his brother had a lot of growing up to do. Deciding on a place to live had been his first step in the right direction, but they hadn't thought he was going to move out of Cedar Valley and into another state. If he had to be honest, he was still bitter about Conner's move.

"I'll believe it when I see it," Adam said, waving off the conversation with a quick, "Better get back to work before the chief suspects we're slacking."

Hearing about Conner moving back, twice in two days, was unnerving. Had his relationship weakened that much with Conner that the guy wouldn't talk to him about returning to Cedar Valley? He would have liked to think they had a strong bond, but it appeared that was no longer the case. He made a mental note to give Conner a call later tonight, after he tucked the kids into bed.

---

11

*H*er shift at school had been shortened by a couple of hours for teacher in-service, which meant that she had some time to herself before having to pick Ava up from daycare. She had once hated leaving Ava at the daycare, until she realized how much Ava enjoyed going. Her daughter seemed to enjoy the interaction with the other kiddos—so much so that lately she fussed when it was time to go home.

Digging through her purse, she pulled her car keys out and unlocked her car. She had gone all day without so much as a drop of caffeine. She had run behind this morning, too late to make a pot of coffee, and Adam had long since left the house, hours before her alarm woke her up.

Pulling her car out of the parking lot, she headed in the direction of the coffee shop downtown. She was more than ready for a hot cup of coffee or two—her body was not used to a lack of caffeine.

Granny Mae's Café sat in the middle of the block where finding a parking spot was a chore in and of itself. Rachel pulled in across the street, thankful for a random old guy leaving the barber shop.

The bell above the door rang when she stepped inside. She had been invited to this place on more than one occasion by Rosie since it had opened two weeks ago, but Rachel had plenty on her plate and no time to stop in to check it out.

The talk of the town had mentioned how cozy and welcoming the place was. They had said it was more of an older lady hangout than it was for anyone else, but Rachel couldn't care less as she walked in the direction of Rosie's wave; she was standing behind the coffee colored counter next to the glass snack display case.

"You finally decided to stop in," Rosie called out, as she turned to grab the other woman's attention from behind the swinging door. Apparently, Rachel's visit was something special, as an older woman walked out wiping her hands on her checkered apron.

"This must be Rachel?" The woman gave Rachel a once over followed with a bright smile that lifted the wrinkles on her face. The woman had a resemblance quite like her own grandmother's with flawless fair skin and light blue eyes.

"Rachel, dear, come here and meet Granny Mae," Rosie said, holding an outstretched hand as she guided Rachel around the length of the counter. "She's the owner."

There was something about Rosie and Granny Mae, like they had something planned. Innocent older ladies were hardly ever as innocent as they seemed. Especially since the café had just opened and Rachel knew they were looking for help—the sign on the door had made that official.

"First of all, I'd like to tell you that it's nice to finally meet you," Granny Mae said, taking hold of Rachel's hand and patting it. "Adam and Tyler are so blessed to have you in their lives."

"Thank you." She didn't know quite what to say. "I'm sure that I'm the one who should be thankful for them."

She wouldn't mention her reasons why. A sweet older lady didn't need to know much more than what the town was saying. Rachel would leave it that way for as long as she could. Having Ava out of wedlock was frowned upon by some, but seemed to be forgiven since coming to Cedar Valley to be with Adam and Tyler.

"Rosie says that you're helping out at the school with the kiddos?" Granny Mae asked, walking over to the shelved pecan pies and pulling one from the bottom. "I'm sure you have your hands full with those young ones. That age always keeps you on your toes, but you would know that with Ava, right dear?"

"Yes, she definitely keeps me going."

The fact that the kids at school were three times the age of Ava didn't change the fact that they kept her busy. A classroom full of six year olds was asking for it, especially lately, when they were getting antsy for their summer break.

"How do you like working there?"

If she had to guess, Granny Mae was hinting around the idea of asking Rachel to work at the café. She wouldn't be able to tell her no, because she loved to bake and she adored Rosie. She would enjoy working alongside Rosie while selling coffee and cinnamon rolls on Thursdays.

"I like it," Rachel said, smiling just enough to make her reply seem as genuine as possible. She really did like working with kids, but after having Ava, she needed a break from the wild and crazy in order to keep her sanity. A change of pace would be appreciated.

"But?"

"But..." It came out more of a hesitation than a question. As though Granny Mae knew she wanted something more, something less noisy and more enjoyable than chasing six year olds around a playground, constantly telling them to be nice to one another, and once in the classroom to use inside voices that they seldom remembered they had.

"What would you say if I asked you to work here?" Granny Mae's eyes lit up just at the thought, and Rachel couldn't possibly tell her no. "You can tell the school that you'll fill in as needed there, but you'll be busy with full time hours here."

Rachel should have talked it over with Adam before coming to a decision, but it all happened so fast and the look on Granny's face at the mention of having Rachel work there... It was too much to wait on or turn down.

Glancing around the café, with the light brown mochas and coffee cups doodled wallpaper bordering the sitting area to the left of the counter, she couldn't ignore how calm the place was. Even with chatter over coffee in the corner across the way, the place was quieter than home and school put together. Plus, the place had a natural cozy feel that was hard to ignore as her eyes ventured the surroundings.

"I heard that you and Tyler love to bake," Granny Mae said, carrying a plated slice of pecan pie toward an older gentleman with a scruffy beard and a gap in his smile who was waiting patiently. "We could always use a baker here, you know?"

Granny Mae was trying too hard, but Rachel wouldn't tell her that. She didn't even need to keep trying. Rachel was sold on the idea when it was first mentioned. Leaving school behind would be a little rough, but after baking for a few days and enjoying the coffeehouse music over the buzzing chatter, Rachel wouldn't regret it.

Looking down at her phone, she thought about calling Adam, but she knew that he'd be happy with whatever she chose to do; as long as she was happy, he was happy. That's the way she felt about him and his work, too. It scared her to think of him fighting fires, and the chances of him getting hurt were high; but knowing that he loved it and enjoyed it, she couldn't make him walk away from it.

"I'll tell you what," Granny Mae said, leaning against the counter as she pulled a piece of scratch paper from beside the register. Granny smiled as she scribbled a list that Rachel couldn't see from a distance, but was sure it involved something along the lines of baking and an offer Rachel once again wouldn't say no to.

"You take this with you," Granny said, handing the paper to Rachel. "Take it home, talk it over with Adam, and let me know tomorrow."

Folding the paper without looking at it, Rachel would

do as she was told. With a friendly wink and wave from Rosie, and a kiss on the cheek, she headed out the door. There wasn't much more that could make her happier than being right here in Cedar Valley with the people she loved.

12

Once home, he knew that he would be far from being able to relax. He had just dropped Tyler off at football practice, so he had just over an hour to help with supper and get things sorted out for the night. He didn't like working all these hours, but he enjoyed what he did. Fighting fires ran hot through his blood and he couldn't imagine giving it up.

Pulling into the driveway, he saw Rachel swinging out front with Ava in her lap. Killing the engine, he climbed out and walked to the porch, taking a seat on the landing.

Rachel's smile welcomed him home before she even said a word. Ava shimmied off her lap and toddled over to him, plopping down in his lap once she made it. "She's been waiting for you all day. Every truck she heard pass by she thought it was you."

"Is that right?" he asked, poking a finger into Ava's plump belly, causing a fit of giggles to erupt from the pacifier-filled mouth of hers. "Guess who's ready to tickle?"

Laying Ava on the porch floor, he allowed the tickle monster to get her, causing hysterics of laughter to echo into the evening calm surrounding them. He heard Rachel's silent chuckle as she sipped from a glass of wine. Her blonde hair fluttered softly against her cheek as a light breeze passed along.

"So, I heard your brother might be moving back soon?" It was more of a question than a statement. He wondered how many people would hear about this before Conner actually said something to him. And he also wondered what the hold-up was.

He knew the shrug he had given in response was a bit cold, but if he were to be honest, it was better than telling her how he truly felt. Which, knowing Rachel, she would get him to open up about it, regardless of how sour he truly was about the whole situation.

From the corner of his eye, he watched her continue to sip from her glass, and what looked like pondering over what to say next, if anything at all. It wasn't how he wanted her to feel. There was no walking on egg shells in this house, not if he could help it. Besides, it wasn't her fault his family was a bit dysfunctional.

"I take it you aren't too happy about it?" she asked, swishing her drink around in her glass as she kept her eyes on him and Ava's tickle fest.

"I can't say that it wouldn't make me happy to have my little bro back home," he finally admitted, pushing aside his differences for a minute. "I just know that he has a lot of growing up to do."

"Huh."

Her one word response was enough evidence to tell him that he had somehow said the wrong thing. It wasn't his choice for his brother to move a whole state away without looking back. He had tried to convince Conner to stay and work out the differences, but his advice had been ignored when Conner's mind was made up.

"What?"

It was her turn to shrug, and if he had to honest, she was a bit cuter when she was upset about something. Her cheeks had a tint of pink, probably from the alcohol, and her eyes—there was something about them that had his attention.

"I don't think anyone should judge him," she said, finishing off the last of her drink. "Besides, he's still young and he shouldn't have to settle."

Had it been that long since he was young and antsy to get out of this town? He hadn't once really taken himself seriously when he had the thoughts of leaving.

"Maybe you're just jealous that you hadn't thought about leaving before he did?"

Taken aback by her accusation, he had no choice but stand on the front porch in complete silence with his jaw damned near on the ground. He didn't know how to answer that without sounding like a spoiled brat... even though he surely was far from that... *and* thirty-four years old. What the heck had he been thinking before getting into this heated discussion with her?

"Okay, I call a truce," he said, holding his hands up in defense. "And for the record, I ain't jealous. He's out there fighting fires in Colorado while I've got this right here."

He wrapped an arm around her and Ava, pulling them close as he planted his lips on each of their foreheads, hoping that it would settle Rachel's spunk. He had to give her credit, she was a force to be reckoned with when it came to what she felt was right.

Pulling the door open with one hand, he guided them into the house with the other. "How about some supper and we can talk about things that make us happy?" he asked, smiling wide in hopes that she'd calmed down. "Like little Ava saying Daddy instead of Mommy."

"Now you're pushing it," Rachel warned, as she walked past him.

Leaving Ava to run wild in the confines of the baby gates, they decided on cooking supper together. Rachel had admitted that she wasn't a very good cook, but he had made the promise that it wasn't a deal breaker. He never believed in having women slave in the kitchen while their men sat in the other room kicking back with a beer in their hands.

"Ty should be home in a half hour or so," he said, glancing at the clock on the stove. "I told him that he could catch a ride with one of his buddies."

He watched Rachel as she peeled the potatoes. Her technique was perfect, unlike his, she didn't gouge half the potato just to get a single peeling off. He took a moment to take a peek at Ava, who was bouncing around to the music of her favorite Sesame Street song.

"What's the big deal about your brother anyway?"

He didn't feel like discussing this with her, not right now. Not like there was much to talk about. The choice had been Conner's and he had taken it without a single hint of hesitation. He'd tried to stop him the last day he was in town, but Conner had his mind made up and there was no stopping a Jacobsen from doing what they wanted.

"He had a tiff with our father," he said, keeping an eye

on the chicken in the pan as it slowly browned. "They hardly ever saw eye to eye, and I think Dad's age was somewhat to blame. He was getting older, refused to give much slack to Conner, and instead of bringing him closer to the fire department here, he shoved him away."

He watched as Rachel rinsed the potatoes and emptied the strainer into the pan. He waited for her to say something, anything, along the lines of the relationship, but she didn't. Instead, she prepared the steamer by pouring a bag full of frozen vegetables in and lighting the fire underneath.

"He hasn't said anything to me about moving back, which is odd, because Iwas the one who had insisted he stay here in Cedar Valley." This wasn't how he'd expected the night to go, but since it was brought up, he had no choice but to talk about it. "I don't think he wanted to work under our father's scrutiny, but he refused to give up the Jacobsen's passion of fighting fires. It left him with no choice but to leave Cedar Valley."

Placing a lid over the chicken as it cooked, he ventured away from the stove and propped himself against the counter. He hated to think that it was because of their father he had lost a close bond with his brother, but that was neither here nor there.

"I don't know what would make him come back here, other than the fact that our father recently retired as chief, which opens up an opportunity for Conner to work here and be free of my father's strict ways," he said, offering her the only logical explanation he could come up with. It only made sense, for the simple fact that Conner couldn't stand their father's strict military ways, which had overseen the fire department for the last twenty-some odd years. Hell, he couldn't blame Conner, he felt the same way about their father, but it was just different with him. "Who'd you hear it from anyway?"

Carrying a plate of lemon-peppered chicken to the table, she said, "Leah was talking about it today while she was at the daycare."

It should have been obvious who she had heard it from. The two of them were inseparable. The best of friends, who, unlike anyone he had ever known, had been through a lot together. "What'd she have to say about it?"

Rachel smiled as she bent over to pick up Ava, who had been standing at the gate, more than ready to eat. "Nothing much. Just that it's all she's heard about since taking on a couple of shifts with Megan at Levy's."

It didn't surprise him that Megan was talking about Conner. They had completed their training the same summer together. Megan, of course, had to continue with more schooling in order to get where she was now— Cedar Valley's finest medic—but that didn't mean she had stopped talking to his brother.

"She says she won't shut up about it, actually," Rachel said, scooping a spoonful of peas onto Ava's tray. "Have they had a thing for each other or something?"

The slam of the screen door directed his attention away from their conversation. Tyler walked in, carrying his football gear, tracking mud in behind him. Adam held a hand up and motioned for Tyler to turn and make his way back to the door, pointing at the mess he'd just made on their clean carpet. Looking from the monster muddied footprints to Rachel, who was already grabbing a rag to clean it up, Adam said, "You have to remember to take your shoes off, bud."

"Sorry, Dad, I wasn't thinking," Tyler said, as he offered to take over clean up—which Rachel gladly handed over.

"Did you eat?" Rachel asked Tyler, making her way back to the kitchen table, where Ava was smashing her peas with balled up fists before cramming them into her mouth.

"No, they wanted to order pizza, but it was getting late. They wanted to get us home on time," Tyler said, tossing the dirtied rag into a nearby bin for dirty laundry. "Dad, we made three touchdowns tonight in practice."

"That's good son," he said, patting him on the back as he slid behind him on his way to his spot. Rachel divied up a spoonful of peas, ignoring Tyler's protest she flopped them onto his plate. He wasn't much for vegetables, something she could relate with. Vegetables had an awkward taste to them. Almost like eating grass. "When's your first game? They get your schedule yet?"

Excitement filled Tyler's face before he climbed out of his chair. Before Adam could holler at him to sit back down and worry later about whatever he was after, Tyler had already managed to pull the schedule from his bag. "Are you going to be able to come to the games, Dad?"

The feeling of being sucker punched in the gut would have felt better than how his son's question had. The question was full of innocence, like any other young child questioning their parent's attendance at something important to them, but his own guilt of picking up extra hours at the station was creeping up on him.

Rather than waiting until after supper to look it over, he held out his hand for the gold colored paper Tyler handed to him. Taking a glance at it, he was relieved to see that most of the games were scheduled for home and they fell on his days off. "You bet. I wouldn't miss a single game."

Making a promise he wasn't sure he could keep had become his weakness as a father. He only wanted what was best for Tyler, and now Ava, and he was willing to do whatever it was to make it happen. It was almost as though his mind was on constant repeat of all the times his father had let him down by not showing up when he had promised he would.

"Tell ya what, let's pin this to the fridge and we'll talk more about it tomorrow," he offered, as he slid his way around the table in order to hang the paper on the fridge. "We'd better eat before the food gets cold. Rachel and I worked hard on this supper."

Offering a wink to Rachel, he said, "But Rachel deserves most of the credit. If it wasn't for her, we'd be having pizza for the third time this week."

Not that they'd had pizza that often this week. He was only making a statement because if it wasn't for Rachel and Ava moving in, he and Tyler would definitely still be roughing it.

13

Clearing the table and putting dishes away, Rachel allowed Adam to tuck the kids in. Tyler had protested that he was getting too old to be tucked in, but Adam had insisted jokingly that as long as he lived under this roof, he'd get tucked in. Tyler had made a face at Rachel, almost as if to say he was calling his dad's bluff, but Rachel egged it on by saying he was probably telling the truth.

She watched as Adam carried Ava off to bed, turning the corner around the stairway banister, climbing each step as he promised she could listen to as much Elmo as she wanted in the morning.

She had everything she needed right here in this house, right here in Cedar Valley. All she needed now was a job that she enjoyed as much as Adam enjoyed his. She thought about the offer from Granny Mae's before she heard Adam whistling, as his heavy footfalls landed on the steps.

Pulling the folded paper from her pocket, she looked it

over as Adam entered the dining room. His eyes landed on the paper before offering her a questioning look. She held it up like it was no big deal and said, "I stopped by Granny Mae's earlier and was offered a job."

His expression changed from worry to excitement. "That's great. Are you going to take it?"

She had wanted to tell Granny Mae that she accepted the offer as soon as it was given to her, but she had thought it best to talk it over with him before making any sudden changes that could possibly affect their schedules. She'd already lost a couple of extra hours a day with him, now that he was picking up the slack at the station. They were down a few guys, so it was something he had no choice but to fill in where there were gaps.

"I told her that I would let her know tomorrow."

Pulled into his arms, she wrapped hers around his neck. "I know that you don't like working at the school as much as you did back in the city, and you know that I'd rather you not work at all, because we could manage just fine," he said, keeping his sincere eyes locked on hers. She knew this, because they had talked about it many times before she finally accepted his offer to move here. He had told her several times that she wouldn't have to work, if what she wanted to do was stay at home with the kids; that he would be fine with that. Before she could rebut what he had already heard her say many times before, he said, "If they offered you a position to bake, I think you should take it. Your baking is the bomb dot com, if I say so myself."

He pressed her against him, leaving a trail of kisses from her earlobe down along the sensitive skin of her neck. Allowing her head to fall back, she forgot what they had even been talking about while thoughts of straddling him right there on the couch rushed in. It had been more than a week since they had last snuck in time for themselves, and now that the kids were in bed and the offer was blatantly in their favor, she refused to keep talking and waste another minute.

Shoving him back, his knees bent against the couch as he fell back, landing with a hard thump in the center of the couch. Straddling each leg over his lap, she teased him with what she knew he couldn't resist. Weaving her hands through his hair, allowing her body to grind against his, she teased him in such a way that he would be begging her to finish him.

His hardened length pressed against her, separated by the thin material of clothing. She fumbled with his buckle, along with his zipper and he stripped her shirt, tossing it into a heaping pile next to the couch. Cupping her breast in his hand, he found her weakness with his mouth, and as he suckled on a nipple, and she was begging him to have his way with her.

His grunt was heard over the deafening rush in her eardrums as he stripped her bare without a struggle. Sweat glistened against his face as she struggled with his zipper, pressed firmly against his erection.

Frustration charged though as he lifted her, and she wrapped her legs around him as he carried her to their bedroom, adjacent to the living room. Catching the door with his foot behind them, Rachel watched as the door closed.

He had his pants unbuckled and down to the floor before he even put her on the bed beneath him. He crawled to the edge of the bed, pulled open the drawer of the night stand, and pulled out a condom. She ripped it from his hand and tossed it out of reach as she crawled on top of him. "We don't need that, do we?" she breathlessly whispered against his skin before being hoisted on top, straddling him once again; she took them into an unconscious stupor.

———

Talking over breakfast about her decision on changing jobs; they welcomed Tyler's input. He had told Rachel, yet again, that when he was old enough, he would come work with her at Granny Mae's and they could bake the best pancakes in the world. Once again, the conversation had ended with a promise not to take too many pancake lovers away from the fire department.

Filling his mug to the brim with coffee, Adam sealed the lid with a quick twist and kissed Rachel on his way out the door. It was his third Saturday pulling a shift at the station, and, though one could say he could stay home with the pager on standby, he disagreed because there was always something going on that needed his attention. He wasn't one to sit at home and ignore it, but then again, he wasn't one to ignore his family either.

"I'm going to be working on an ad for the paper today," he promised Rachel, offering another kiss before making his way out the door. "I'll be making sure we hire at least two people by mid-week."

Following Rachel's blown kiss out the door, he turned and shut it. It had been too long since he had enjoyed a Saturday at home with Rachel and the kids. He knew without her telling him so, that it was getting redundant, with him working so many hours through the week and then come the weekend, still having to pull another full shift or two.

Backing out of the driveway, he pulled his phone from the side pocket of his carpenter shorts and dialed his brother. Some would call it desperation, he called it determination. "Hey, bro," he said as soon as he heard Conner on the other end of the line. "Whatcha got goin' on today?"

Trying to make friendly conversation had become tedious where their bond was concerned. Left aside due to his move, Adam didn't quite know how to start a conversation with him. It sucked because they had once been close. Not terribly close, but close enough to have a decent conversation without the awkwardness.

"Not a lot. I got the day off so I'm getting ready to take off and hit some trails."

Glancing at the clock on the stereo, he realized that it was before seven there in Colorado. Another thing that had changed since Conner had moved. The kid hadn't enjoyed mornings, and had spent his days playing video games until he was forced to shut them off. He hadn't thought his brother had it in him to pursue any kind of fitness, let alone running along the mountain trails.

"Wish I could say the same," he said, grumbling over the fact he couldn't. "Except for the trails part. It's been a while since I've run outdoors."

It was kind of upsetting to admit that he was somewhat out of shape. As a firefighter, the last thing you wanted to be was out of shape. There'd come a time that it would kick him the ass. The thought actually scared the shit out of him. Not that he was too out of shape to handle his job, but he had to admit it wouldn't hurt to get back into running.

"I'll have to whip you back in shape if I come back, old man."

"Hey, about that, I've heard from quite a few people that you're thinking about coming back," he said, trying to keep his tone calm. "When were you gonna let me know about it?"

Awkward silence hung between them, and he knew his brother hadn't wanted him to find out. Hesitation could be heard in Conner's voice when he said, "I'm not sure I'm coming back."

"Come on, man, you can't be serious right now."

So much for keeping his anger under control. His cheeks flared red with heat as he thought about his brother keeping him out of the loop. "What is it?"

"What is what?"

"What's keeping you from coming back home?"

Failing miserably at keeping his anger to a minimum and his tone calm, Adam blew out a ragged breath before saying, "I didn't call to hear excuses, bro. I called to ask, because we need help here. We're down a few guys and I'm struggling to keep the shifts full."

As desperate as it sounded, he couldn't care less. They had to break up this bullshit between them. Whatever pissing match had happened was well over and gone by now. There was no pissing match 'where he was concerned, and he wasn't going to let his brother believe there was. Hell, he wasn't even sure if there ever really had been one.

"So, you're in charge now?"

Grunting, Adam gripped the steering wheel until his

hands turned pale. In his eyes, it didn't matter who was in charge of the station. All that mattered was the community being protected. The medics did their job, the deputies did theirs, and the fire department was barely staying afloat.

"Tell me why that matters?"

Pulling the truck into an empty spot near the station, he slammed into park. This wasn't how he had wanted the conversation to go. He wasn't sure how smooth he had originally thought it would have gone, but he had definitely thought it would have gone a helluva lot smoother than this.

"It doesn't."

Brushing a stressed hand through his hair as he looked in the rearview mirror, he could see the wear and tear from the job. His hair was thinning, his eyes were tired, and his body was exhausted. Pulling regular shifts upon double shifts was getting to him. He would do whatever it took to get men on board at Cedar Valley Fire Department.

"Look, man, I didn't call to cause an uproar," he said, damned near betting that his brother was blowing him off. "I just heard that you were talking about moving back home and thought I'd talk to you about it."

He wasn't going to waste any more time on this conversation. It was pointless and nothing was going to change his brother's mind. Regardless if he was really coming back home or not, he wasn't going to tell Adam. That was fine with him. It was whatever.

"I guess I'll just talk to you later, then."

Without waiting for his brother to confirm the conversation was done, he hit the end key and tossed his phone onto the dash of his pickup. Slamming his hand against the steering wheel, he cursed all things unworthy.

He couldn't guarantee he wouldn't lose his shit, but if things didn't change at the station, he promised himself he would walk away, no matter how bad the department needed him to stay.

---

14

*S*hortly after dropping Ava off at daycare, she called the school to let them know she wouldn't be there today. She had given them two weeks' notice the day after she had told Granny Mae that she would take the job, and had only a few days left. Baking was her passion, and what was the saying? Find a job you love and you'll never work another day in your life?

She was looking forward to living up to that. Being able to spend more time in the mornings with Ava, practicing her ABCs and one, two, threes, meant the world to her. She couldn't help but think of all the valuable time she had long since missed when she had begun her mornings at seven and ended her days after four.

The bell above the door chimed as she walked in. The first person she noticed was Leah, who was more pregnant than the last time she had seen her, a couple of weeks ago. They hadn't been able to spend much time together, with Tyler's practice and Adam working crazy hours; she wanted to spend as much of her time at home as she could.

"I was hoping you would be here today," Leah said, waddling her way toward Rachel, carrying a paper in her hand. "Rosie mentioned that you'll be working here now?"

Taking the paper from Leah, she looked it over. Of course it was her list of what she wanted for her baby shower. A baby bump cake, with a pink polka dot dress and a black bow. A special note in parenthesis stated that the boobs had to be ginormous because hers were. Rachel chuckled at the thought of making this cake for Leah.

"I know, it's a lot of work to hammer you with," Leah said, pointing at the list.

"And don't forget it's still a few months away," Rachel added. Making note that Leah also wanted frosted cookies, shaped according to baby related things. Another note in parenthesis stating that Rachel would know what to do.

"Yeah, I know, but I'm really hoping these last few months fly by," she said, rubbing a hand around her swollen belly. Her baby bump had grown—nearly doubled—since the last time Rachel had seen her. She tried not to laugh, because she knew how miserable pregnancy could be when you're swollen and feel fat, along with being miserable from heartburn.

"She'll be here before you know it," she said, rubbing a hand against Leah's belly. She bent over and whispered, "Isn't that right, little miss?"

"Oh, boy, please don't let Liam here you say that," Leah said, a moan escaped her lips as she mumbled something under her breath. "He swears that our baby's a boy."

"Well, he's going to be disappointed when he finds out

you're having a girl," she said, giving an extra rub to the baby bump.

Leah laughed when Rosie walked in from the back with a stern look on her face. "Lord knows we don't need another Spencer boy. We need us a sweet little miss who will love to cook with Grammy."

Taking a seat at the counter, Rachel pulled a chair closest to her out for Leah to climb onto. Reaching for the tip jar near the register, she said, "We'll just have to take some bets on what this little one will be."

Rosie pulled the jar out of reach, tucking it behind the register out of Rachel's view. "No, there'll be no betting on the gender of a baby. Lord knows we'll be happy with whatever gender the babe will be."

Rachel shrugged. "As long as it's healthy and loves her aunt Rach, that's all that matters."

Amid laughter at her insinuation that *it* was a her, Leah grabbed a pen and wrote down the date that she would find out. That way, Rachel could be there to throw a mini celebration if *it* in fact was a girl.

"So, enough about me and this baby," Leah said, twisting toward Rachel in the chair. "How are things going for you?"

She didn't like to brag, but she had a lot of things that were going great. She couldn't be more thankful for the way things were. "Better, now that Granny Mae offered me a job here."

"You know those kiddos are going to miss you," Leah said, shaking a finger in her direction. She was pretty sure they would, too, but they could see her any time around town. "But you'll have it made here. Granny Mae is the sweetest old lady ever."

"I heard that," Granny Mae's voice hollered from the kitchen.

Leah cupped a hand around her mouth and whispered, "She has really good hearing for an old lady too."

Laughing, Rachel folded the paper Leah had given her in half and tucked it under her keys.

"I heard that, too."

Granny Mae shuffled out of the back with a tray full of food. Rachel glanced around. The place was empty. Not a single person was here for breakfast. "What are you going to do with all that food?"

Placing the tray in the center of them, Granny Mae huffed. Handing out a plateful each, Rachel politely refused. "Don't be silly. I didn't cook all of this for nothing. Besides, it's good food if I say so myself."

Knowing that she couldn't turn it down, she grabbed the plate and stuck a fork into the sausage, sliding it through maple syrup before it landed in her mouth. She loved Granny Mae's pancakes, and the thought of Tyler's plan came to mind.

"You know that Tyler wants to work here with me when he's old enough?"

"You don't say?" Rosie asked, smiling with a wink. "I knew that boy liked to bake since the day he bragged about baking with you."

"He says that we're going to make the best pancakes in town," Rachel informed them. Laughing at Granny Mae's reaction. Of course, no one would be able to top Granny Mae's Café with their pancakes. "He and Adam debate about it almost every time the word pancake is mentioned. Poor Ava had no idea what she started the other morning, requesting pancakes for breakfast."

"Well, heck, might as well let the boy dream," Granny Mae offered a devious grin before filling her mouth with a forkful of scrambled eggs.

The breakfast tasted delicious, especially since Rachel had forgotten to grab a bite to eat before leaving the house this morning. Making sure the kids had their breakfast, and Tyler had his cold lunch packed, she hadn't worried about herself. Another privilege of motherhood she was getting used to.

"So, have you thought about what you'll bake for the café?" Rosie asked while Granny Mae busied herself clearing plates from the counter. "We love homemade pies and cookies, don't we Mae?"

"Yes, we do!" Granny Mae was shuffling around behind the swinging doors, busied with dishes and scrubbing skillets, but Leah was right, the woman wouldn't miss a beat with her hearing. "Say, Rachel, how about making some of those whatchamacallits..." her face twisted in confusion as she racked her brain trying to think of what she was referring to. Giving up a short minute later, she waved an annoyed hand and went back to work behind the scenes.

"When do you start here?" Rosie asked, stirring the silence in the café as Rachel zoned out thinking about what she could bake for the customers at the café.

"I'm not sure... I guess we never talked about it."

"She can start as soon as she wants to," Granny Mae hollered from the kitchen. "I was leaving it for her to decide."

"Okay, then," Rosie laughed, pouring another round of sweet tea. "I guess that answers that."

Rachel glanced at a nearby calendar on the wall. She

assumed it wouldn't matter when she started, as long as she was done at the school—give or take a few days.

"I can start Monday." That would give her a fresh start to a new week. New job, new week, and a whole new opportunity. Something she would look forward to all weekend.

Leah slid off the chair, grabbing her wallet and her keys. "Thank you Gran for the breakfast, but I have to get going. I have a doctor's appointment in Rockford at eleven-forty."

She wished that she could go with her, but knew that if Liam wasn't busy he would end up going. She missed their times together. They had once been inseparable. Now they were busy playing catch up as they lived their own lives, which thankfully intertwined on days like today.

Wrapping her arms around Leah, she fought back the tears that stung her eyes. As though Leah knew, she whispered, "Don't start that. We'll both be in trouble. Once I start, I can't stop."

Laughing, she squeezed Leah one last time for good measure and released her. Wiping a stray tear from her cheek, Rachel laughed through a trembling lip. She couldn't help the emotion that overcame her when she thought of how things had been and how they were now. So much had changed in the last year, for the better without complaints, but it still felt like they had parted along the way.

"Drive safe," Rosie called after Leah, who in turn smiled and waved, blowing them a kiss as she walked out the door. "That girl worries me, ever since her car accident."

Rachel patted Rosie's hand, a simple reassurance that she could relate to how she felt. It had been quite the year they'd had. She hadn't been sure how they all managed to make it out alive. With the car accident, the fire, and everything else between, she was just thankful that they were all here and doing well.

Grabbing her paper, along with her keys, she called out to Granny Mae, "Thanks again for breakfast, Granny. I'll be here Monday morning."

Granny Mae pushed through the dividing swinging doors. Pointing the spatula she was using to make lunch for the noon rush, she told Rachel, "I don't want you here no sooner than ten. No need to spoil your time with that babe of yours. I'll have this all squared away so it can become your baking station."

Rachel's eyes drifted over the location Granny Mae was showing her. In the back of the kitchen, there was a wide open area with shelves and plenty of counter space. Plenty of room to mix up batches and batches of cookies or muffins, whichever was on the list for the day, and there wouldn't be a single thing she wouldn't love above working at Granny Mae's Café.

15

*P*ulling the stack of applications from the desk, he flipped through until he found one that stuck out at him. "I'll be damned."

Had he known his brother had applied right before his father had retired, he would have tried harder to get him on the team. For whatever reason, his father didn't want Conner in the service, Adam couldn't care less.

Picking up his phone, he dialed his father and waited a good minute and several rings for him to pick up. Finally, his gruff voice wheezed into the phone, out of breath and Adam knew the cigarettes were catching up to him. "Yeah."

Hello to you, too, Adam wanted to say, but refused to let it bother him. "Hey, Dad, how's it going?" Since his retirement, his father's mood had deteriorated. Not sure whether the guy missed working, or if he just wasn't enjoying retirement for whatever reason, Adam wouldn't know. His father was a conservative man, keeping his feelings on lock-down and his emotions in check. Years in the military, along with years with the department, could be blamed. But that was a discussion for another day. Right now, Adam wanted to hear his reasons for not hiring Conner. When his father grunted in response to how things were going, Adam said, "I called to talk to ya about this pile of applications."

"Heck, son, I gave that up a while ago," his father said, sounding a bit harsh.

No shit. Adam bit his tongue. It was obvious that his father had given it up, way before his retirement even. The list of things that had been left undone still hung over Adam's head, on top of empty shifts and the threat of the department going downhill. Part of him wanted to throw in the towel, but the other knew that wasn't the kind of guy he was. He couldn't stand back and watch it burn, especially since it was his family name that had lit the match.

"I didn't know Conner had applied," Adam said, tapping a pen against his brother's application, waiting for his father's response. "Did you know that he'd applied?"

Another grunt told Adam that he was stepping across a line that he shouldn't be crossing, but he didn't really care. He was a grown man now; his father's military ways couldn't scare him into backing down from what was right and wrong, when it came to how his father ran things around here. Hell, the whole time growing up, he'd idolized the man because of everything he had done, oblivious later on to the reasons Conner wanted to leave the state. If there was any kind of revelation, this would be it.

"No, I didn't know that he'd applied."

Tapping against the top page of the application, Adam

focused on the date. It would make sense that his father had ignored it, since the date was two weeks prior to his retirement. But still, it was his son. Didn't he want the Jacobsen sons to carry on what he took pride in?

"The application is dated two weeks before your retirement," Adam said, knowing that his words were rocking the boat. "Is there a reason why you didn't hire him?"

"Watch your tone with me, son," his father said, warning him with a tone of his own. "I have my reasons, but I won't share them with you."

He should leave well enough alone. Heck, he shouldn't have even called the old man. His mother had told him that his moods were unpredictable lately. She had taken him to the therapist and she had made it clear that he wasn't violent with her—that's all Adam cared about.

"The department needs people. I think you had an idea that the department was going under. People were jumping off, including you."

"What'd I say about that tone, boy?"

Anger rattled the old man's lungs, sending him into another coughing fit. It wasn't like Adam to get into arguments with his father, but he wanted answers and he wanted them right now. It all made sense. If Conner knew that their father wouldn't hire him, their father was the reason he left state. The reason he no longer had a close enough bond to the only brother he had, aside from the ones in uniform.

"He wasn't ready. He was too young and immature."

"He was the same age I was," he rebutted. "I wasn't too mature back then, either."

Another grunt, followed by the flick of a lighter, his

father said, "You were going places. He wasn't. He didn't know his head from his ass. Still doesn't."

It wasn't his business, what made his father and brother not see eye to eye, but this conversation made it obvious that his father had resentment against Conner. For whatever reason, it was unclear, but he knew it would wash out into the open before too much longer.

"Well, I still don't understand why you wouldn't let him in the service," Adam said, stacking the applications in a manila folder before locking the office behind him. He had been here most of the day. It was time to go home and relax, try to enjoy the night with his family.

"I won't have this conversation with you."

"That's fine, because I'm bringing him back to Cedar Valley," he said, his teeth grit together. "And he'll work in this department regardless of what you think."

THE CALL HAD GONE HORRIBLY awry. He wanted to call and apologize to his mother for having to put up with the man's anger afterward. It wasn't like them to fight and argue, especially over the phone. But it was obvious that his father had it out for Conner and wasn't telling anyone the truth. What had Conner done so wrong growing up that his father seemed to resent him for it?

Dialing Rachel, she answered on the second ring. He refused to go home worked up; it wasn't fair to her or the kids. "Hey, babe."

"Hey," she said, her voice sounded sweet and he wished he hadn't called his father, so he would be driving home instead of the opposite way. "I just gave Ava a bath. Supper will be done in a bit. I made your favorite."

He hated to back out on supper with her and the kids. He wanted nothing more than the family life, but between the job and his father, he needed to step away for a bit.

"I'm sorry, I won't be home for supper," he said, hoping she wouldn't be too upset. "I've had a rough day, so I'm heading to Levy's for a bit. I need to take some time and clear my head."

Hesitation told him that she wasn't sure about letting him go. "Is everything okay? Do you need me to take the kids to your parents for the night?"

The last place he wanted the kids to go was to his parents, no offense to his mother. The kids didn't need to be in the mix of all of this. "No, I'll be home in a couple of hours."

"Are we okay?"

Her words gutted him. To think that she had even an ounce of speculation that this was about them... "Yes, babe, we're fine. This has nothing to do with us, or the kids. I just need to clear my mind before I come home."

"What happened?" her question was filled with concern. He loved the way she was. The type to try to solve every problem, but this one was on him. No one but he and his brother could figure this out. "I think you should take some time off. We could go to the beach, or rent a cabin out at the lake."

"Babe, I'll be okay. It's just, work got to me a bit today and I need a couple of beers to unwind." Knowing she was still processing through what could have possibly happened, he said, "I promise. Everything's okay."

"Okay, if you promise. Be careful," she said, the sweet voice he loved to hear. "I love you."

"I love you, too."

Pulling into Levy's, he wasn't sure if Liam would be working tonight or not. He needed to unwind. Shoot some pool, kick back a couple of beers, and shoot some shit with the guys. Later, he'd go home and everything would be fine. He'd call his brother tomorrow and tell him, more like plead with him, to come back home.

The bar was crowded for a weeknight. Walking in, he was relieved to see Liam and a few of their buddies hanging out around the counter. Holding a hand out, Liam gripped his, pulling him in close for a bro hug. They'd become better friends over the years, but were closer now than ever before because of their girls.

"You put a ring on that finger yet?" Liam joked.

"Nah, too much shit's been going on lately."

"That's too bad," Liam said, walking around the counter to grab Adam a drink, but Megan shooed him out of the area before he could reach the cooler.

"You're not working tonight," she said, smacking him with a towel. "It's my night to rock this place."

Liam scuttled away with a defeated, devious grin on his face. Giving her a thumbs up, he turned back toward Adam. "I think she's got the hots for Conner. Can you imagine?"

"Man, I've heard enough." He really didn't care who had the hots for Conner, whether it be Megan, or Granny Mae, he couldn't care less. He tapped a couple of quarters into the jukebox and selected a few songs, making a vow to leave by nine. It was quarter to seven now.

"Just think, it might get him to come back here," Liam jabbed. "Do you think he knows?"

Shrugging, Adam reached for a pool stick from the stand and racked the balls. The last thing he wanted to concern himself with was Megan O'Brien and his brother. Megan was too good for his brother. She knew what she wanted in life, where his brother didn't exactly know which day of the week it was.

Breaking the balls, it occurred to him that his father had said the same exact damned thing, which had caused him to get pissed off. What the hell was wrong with him?

"Looks like I've got solids," Liam said, chalking his stick before lining up his shot. "So, you still looking for volunteers?"

Swiping away the foam that had dripped onto his goatee, Adam nodded. "We're always looking. Know anyone that'd be interested?"

"If you hire women, I'll join," Megan said, walking around the table to hand him another beer.

"I have no problem hiring women." Hell, if a woman could do the job, it didn't make a difference what gender they were. And if he was being honest, Megan had an aptitude for the job. She already had Paramedic under her belt; why not allow her the chance to join fire and rescue?

When she didn't walk away, he made his shot and looked back at her. Standing with her arms crossed over her fully blossomed chest, she was waiting for him to take her up on the offer.

"Wait... you're serious?"

He looked back at Liam, who slightly shrugged before taking another drink from his bottle. He couldn't remember the last time they had a woman on the squad, let alone the last time a woman took the training.

She was a bad ass, everyone in town knew it. Hell, all of the guys knew when she showed up on scene, shit got real and was going to be taken care of. She was a helluva paramedic who didn't falter where the job was concerned.

"All right," he said, nodding in her direction before lining up his shot. "Be at the station Monday at eight a.m. We'll see what you can do."

"I'll be there."

Liam's face said it all.

"What?"

"I got nothin'," Liam said, holding his hands and beer up in defense.

"Your face expression didn't look like nothing."

With a slight shrug and the pocketing of the eight ball to conclude the first game, Liam made sure Megan was out of ear shot before he said, "You didn't really just offer her a job, did you?"

"I guess we'll find out come Monday, won't we?"

16

*H*e had kept his promise. She had been sitting on the couch, watching Frozen for the umpteenth time this week, when he walked through the back door. "Hey, babe," he called out, finding his way through the maze of scattered toys.

Ava stirred in her lap, squeezing out of her arms to run to his. She was more than happy to have him home. Ava had a few more teeth pushing through, hence the late night.

With her eyes red and swollen, Ava flung her arms around Adam's neck, hanging on him like the little monkey she was. Rachel couldn't help but swoon over how great Adam was with her.

She watched him travel through the overcrowded living room with Ava, unsure how he managed to not stub his toe or step on building blocks. She would have had it all picked up if she hadn't spent the last few hours cradling a screaming child.

"Frozen again?" Adam asked, pointing to the television. Rachel held up three fingers and tried her best to smile. "I have no idea who loves Frozen in this house."

"Me!" Ava said, raising her arms above her head. The medicine Rachel had given her after supper was finally kicking in, taking away all signs of painful gums except for the watery eyes and the red face.

Adam carefully lifted her as he stood from the chair. "What do you say we watch the rest of this tomorrow so we can get a good night's sleep?"

Without a fuss or a whimper, Ava snuggled against his chest, almost as though she agreed that it was past her bed time. Rachel stood to follow them, making sure that no matter how tired she was, they didn't break their nightly routine.

Their nightly routine consisted of two stories and a silly song, credit given to Adam for being so creative. Rachel couldn't take credit for the song Adam and Ava sang night after night as she watched on in awe.

Closing the door behind them, they walked down the hall to check on Tyler. Tyler was growing like a weed, which meant that he was becoming a young man. He no longer liked to be tucked in, but that hadn't stopped Adam, or Rachel for that matter, of stopping by his room and wishing him a goodnight. Closing his door to just a crack, Adam turned to Rachel and said, "Ten going on eighteen. I'm not sure I'm ready."

Rachel wrapped her arms around his neck, looked him in the eyes, and said, "No rushing it. There's still plenty of time."

She had seen the way Adam and Tyler bonded. They were the perfect father and son duo. Unlike any father and child relationship she had ever witnessed, Adam actually cared, and he proved it every day.

The weight of the world was on his shoulders. The tension in his muscles was obvious as they hugged in the hallway, and her hand glided over his shoulder blade. If she could take away the stress he was facing day in and day out, lord knew she would.

Swept off her feet, Adam carried her down the stairs. Afraid that she was going to fall, she held tight to his neck. "Relax, I've got you."

His words reassured her, but the thought of falling still rattled her fears. "I do this for a living, you know?"

Relaxing only a smidge, she asked, "Sweeping women off their feet and carrying them down the stairs?"

Grunting, he set her down on her feet at the base of the stairs. "Worked with you, didn't it?"

There were a lot of things that worked for her when it came to Adam. The way his personality beamed in their conversations; the way he cracked jokes to cheer her up, and the way his eyes said so much even when he couldn't. She had known about the death of Tyler's mother, about the troubling calls Adam had been on with the department, and the overwhelming hurdle of raising a child alone.

Grabbing hold of his hand, she pulled him toward the couch. Tapping her foot along the base of the couch, she told him to have a seat. With a questioning look, he did as she asked. She climbed behind him, straddling his back as she sat down on the couch. Gently, she pushed him forward, moving her hands along the smooth oversized, over-tensed muscles of his back.

He tilted his neck against the pull of his muscle. "Is there anything you can't do?"

Laughing, she pressed her thumbs into the depth of his shoulder and circled against the knots. "I can think of a few things I couldn't do."

"Oh, yeah, what's that?" he asked, grunting against the tightness of his muscle.

"Well, first of all, I couldn't do what you do," she said, knowing that for a fact. She had seen the kind of things firemen do, and regardless of how great the job, she would never in a million years be able to pull that job off. "Second, I couldn't have faced all you have dealt with and come out stronger for it. I would have long since collapsed and given up."

It was a touchy subject, she knew that, but she felt that he needed to hear how much she looked up to him. How much everyone around here looked up to him. He had gone through so much, had been blindsided, and yet, here he was, stronger and still a man of faith.

The shrug of his shoulders pulled against her thumbs. "I'm no superhero. I don't have capabilities that other men don't," he said, so matter-of-fact, with a tone she had never heard before. "I just do what I hope any man would do or any brother of mine in the department would do. Given any situation, you have to do what's right. You can't give up. Not when there are others who depend on you to keep going."

She knew he was no longer talking about Tyler, but now of the community. He had given this community so much, and likewise for them. There were so many supporters of the department, and even more support for him and Tyler.

He relaxed against her legs, she continued circling her thumbs into the tense muscles, and changed the subject. "I took the job at the Granny Mae's."

"I'm sorry, I know you've wanted to tell me about that for a while now," he said, turning toward her, resting his bent knee against the front of the couch. "You'll be baking, right?"

"That's what Granny Mae hired me to do," she said, smiling down at him. "Thanks to Rosie, who mentioned how great a baker I am."

She hadn't thought of herself as an expert at baking. There were plenty of others around here that Granny could choose to fill in the baker's position, not that she would argue with her decision—it had gotten her out of sitting in a classroom all day.

"Rosie knows good baking, with no exception to yours."

"Aww, now you're just being too sweet," she said, nudging him in the arm. "Turn around and let me finish the massage I started."

"That's not the only thing you started," he said, giving her a sly wink with a finger pointed downward. Laughing, he did as she said, while she sat with a bemused look on her face as she wondered when he had become such a horn dog. When she remained quiet, he glanced back at her and smiled. "You know what they say about massages, right?"

Slapping his arm, she said, "I know what they say about dirty old men."

"Hey now, I may be dirty, but I'm not old," he said, more of a growl than of words.

"Yet."

Spinning around, he now faced her on his knees and tackled her against the cushion. She was pinned and unable to fight back or squirm her way out from under him. He trailed his lips down the side of her neck as she squirmed and arched her back beneath him. "I'll show you old man." His breath warm against her neck, his words mumbled as his lips pressed on.

She may have been too tired not that long ago, but right now, with her body pressed against his and nowhere to go, she was more awake than ever.

IF THERE WAS one thing she was good at, it was baking cookies. She wouldn't ever have imagined baking for a living, but she wasn't complaining. Granny Mae's was the perfect place. They were in the middle of town, next to the old post office, and sat adjacent to the small Ma and Pa thrift store.

Flipping the mixer on, Rachel heard the bell above the door ring and Granny Mae holler for her to come out front. She had to meet someone. Wiping her hands off with her apron, Rachel pushed through the swinging dividers and walked over to the spot Granny Mae was standing, talking to a strawberry blonde who looked familiar.

"Rach, have you met Megan?"

Of course, that's why she looked familiar. She was Rosie's granddaughter—the bad-ass paramedic all the guys talked about.

"Not officially, but I've heard about her," Rachel said, smiling as she extended a hand over the counter to shake

Megan's hand. She was gorgeous. "It's nice to finally meet you."

"Hey, Meg," Rosie called out from the other end of the counter. "You're not serious about joining the fire department, are you?"

Rachel glanced at Megan and Rosie, debating whether or not to go back to baking. Her dough was well mixed by now, if not all over the floor and walls.

"Well, I mentioned to Adam the other night that I would love to join," Megan said, taking a seat closer to her grandmother. Rachel could see the distaste of the thought on Rosie's face. "I told Adam that I'd be in on Monday to see what I can do."

A strawberry blonde curl fell loose from the holder and lay against her tan skin. Megan was everything the guys talked about. Rachel hadn't known her before now. She didn't technically know her now, but having her sit in front of her, Rachel could understand why the guys talked.

"I don't think you should," Rosie pleaded, her voice full of concern. "I just don't think it's safe."

"Grandma," Megan said, reaching for Rosie's hand. "The department needs me."

She wasn't lying. Rachel had seen the stress piled on Adam for the last couple of weeks, and she had a feeling he would end up going down if something didn't change soon.

As if Megan needed Rachel's input, she turned her attention in her direction and said, "Rachel, tell her how badly they need help."

"I know they need help," Rosie said, her voice stern. "I just don't think..."

"She'll be in good hands," Rachel said, whether or not it was her place to say anything in regards to Rosie's wishes. Making sure she didn't seem disrespectful, she said, "Adam would make sure of her safety. All of their safety."

Megan's blue eyes lit up, brightened by the dark outline of flawlessly drawn on makeup. She mouthed *Thank you* and Rachel smiled.

"I'd better get back there," she said, pointing toward the backroom where the sound of an overworked mixer whirred in the distance. "I'm sure my dough is plenty mixed by now."

It had been left for a few minutes unsupervised, but it was fine. The chocolate chips were seamlessly mixed within the dough, without a single mess anywhere.

The wooden swinging door opened and Rosie walked into the back room. Her eyebrows were drawn together and she had a tight-lipped expression as she leaned against the counter next to Rachel's baking space. Crossing her arms in front of her, she said, "She's my only grandchild and I don't want anything to happen to her." Before Rachel could say a word, she said, "I know the department needs help. Wes and Edward talk about it every day. I just don't want her to get hurt or overdo it. She's such a go getter and I don't want her to take on too much."

Rachel wasn't quite sure what to say. The department did need volunteers, a lot of them. Adam was struggling to keep shifts full and crews ready for the tones to drop. But she also knew what it was like to worry about something happening to the one you love. She felt that unease daily when Adam left for work.

"I know that Adam needs volunteers," Rosie said, glancing at Rachel before saying, "but I'm not okay with her joining."

Rachel wasn't sure what to say. There wasn't really anything she could say right now to change Rosie's mind. As though Rosie knew this, she turned to Rachel, grabbed her hand and said, "I need you to talk to Adam. Tell him not to hire Megan. Do whatever it takes to keep Megan out of those fires. Please?"

For the first time in a long time, Rachel was at a loss for words. A true conflict between what was needed and what was wanted. Megan had no doubts that she'd be hired on, and Adam, even though he hadn't said anything to her about Megan wanting to join, would hire her in a heartbeat. He respected the O'Brien family and ran with Megan on medical calls. It would take a lot more than Rachel's words to persuade him to change his mind.

Rosie turned, and no sooner than she entered the room, she was gone. Leaving Rachel with conflicted thoughts on whether or not Megan should join the department.

17

*S*undays brought on family dinners at his parents' house. This wasn't Rachel's first Sunday dinner, but it would be her first where there was tension among the table.

Adam had called his father and apologized relentlessly for arguing over something silly. It made no difference why his father hadn't hired Conner. That was between the two of them. It had nothing to do with him, or the service.

His father had grunted an acceptance of the apology, but he knew his father would still be worked up about it. It would make for an interesting night.

Loading Ava into her car seat, he clicked her buckle and handed her favorite stuffed animal to her. The trip would be short, but since she hadn't had a nap, he estimated it'd take her less than a minute on the road before her eyes closed and she was sound asleep.

No sooner than they pulled out of the driveway and headed in the direction of his parents, he saw her reflection in the rearview, peacefully sleeping with her stuffed puppy tucked tightly against the side of her face.

"Did you know that Rosie doesn't want Megan to join the department?" Rachel asked, after a silent couple of minutes of fumbling with the zipper flap on her purse. She hadn't been her normal talkative self since her last shift at Granny Mae's, and he couldn't figure out why. But now, this question might explain it.

"No, I hadn't heard that." He hadn't had time to stop into the cafe, let alone talk much with anyone, including Rosie. The thought of talking to her before Monday hadn't crossed his mind. Until now.

"She doesn't want Megan joining, because she's afraid of something happening to her," Rachel explained the conversation she'd had with Rosie at the cafe, which all made sense. Megan was her only grandchild and like a daughter to Rosie. She wasn't going to let anything happen to her, but neither would he. "I can understand what she means."

The words were like a punch in the gut. He knew that his job wasn't a walk in the park. There were times when things got ugly, but hearing Rachel's words confirmed what he had long since shoved aside. Rachel had expressed her concern when they first began dating, but like everything else, he had promised to be careful as he told her how long he had been in the service and how well he did his job. He had known at that time it wasn't enough to settle her worries, and hearing them now, when they spoke of Rosie's, hit him hard.

"I know," he said, reaching for her hand and giving it a gentle squeeze. He wasn't good at calming these sorts of worries. He could only promise to do his job the best he could, making sure that everyone, including himself, came home every night after their shift ended. "I'll have a talk with Rosie."

Knowing this wouldn't solve the worry, he changed the subject. "Ty, you'll need to tell Gramps about your touchdown. He and Wes couldn't make it to the game because they were on their fishing adventure."

Tyler's games had become a favorite past-time of the old men—his grandfather and Wes. Talk among the guys had become less about sports on television and more about the local school kids' home games.

Tyler had scored a touchdown when his team had least expected it. He had zigged when defense zagged and slid around outstretched arms, outrunning the majority of the opposing team. The touchdown had been the win they were looking forward to.

"Do you think Gramps will want to play catch?"

With a gentle shrug and a grin, Adam said, "You'll have to ask him."

The old man was more fit than some men half his age. The fact that a seventy year old could still throw pigskin without throwing out his shoulder or pulling a muscle said something. Hell, the old man tried to talk his father into letting him in the service a couple of years back. His father had gotten a chuckle out of the conversation, but Adam knew it wasn't a joke. His grandfather had been serious as a heart attack.

Rachel's facial expression told him that she'd believe it when she saw it. Adam shrugged and said, "Wait and see."

Pulling into the drive, Adam's truck crawled to stop behind his grandfather's 50's Buick. That thing was still sharp looking, with not a single scratch or dent in it. His grandfather had kept it in pristine condition and swore the engine still purred like a cat. Adam had no doubts about that.

Piling out of the truck, Tyler grabbed his football and headed for the house, leaving Rachel and Adam fending for themselves as they grabbed Ava and the side dishes they'd promised to bring.

"You didn't hit my Beaut, did ya?" his grandfather called out from the front of the truck, a smile cracked his wrinkled face.

"Hey there, Gramps," Adam said, bringing one arm around the man's shoulders while holding on tight to Ava. "You know I wouldn't."

"She still turns over on the first try," Edward said, motioning his hand as though he were turning the key in the ignition. "Purrs just like a..."

"Cat?"

Leading the family into the house, Edward patted Adam's shoulder, "Atta boy."

It hadn't taken long for Ava to catch the attention as they made their way inside through the back door. Gramps still had Adam's attention, talking about motors and how old he had been the first time he had seen a Buick like the one parked in the drive.

There wasn't a single thing that changed from this conversation and the last his grandfather had with him. Talking about cars was his grandfather's specialty. The man had been the town mechanic for the majority of his life, long before he was Tyler's age. Gramps' talks were always something to look forward to.

Ava squirmed in his arms before he agreed to set her down, allowing her to run off after Tucker, the family dog who was well into his late years of life. The dog was still laid back and friendly, and loved the children's attention.

"Hon," Rachel said, patting his arm before saying, "I'm going to help your mother with dinner."

He nodded and smiled as he watched her hips sway on her way to the kitchen. "You've got quite the woman there," his grandfather said, nudging him with a playful elbow.

"Yeah, she's great," Adam said, still watching her as she set the table in the dining room. He was a lucky man to have such an incredible woman like Rachel in his and Tyler's life. His thoughts were continuously spinning like broken records, circling around Rachel and Ava. But if anything was definite, it was how thankful he was they had come together and for Rachel's lack of hesitation when he had offered her a place to call home. He needed her more than he'd ever needed anyone.

"Hey," his father walked into the back room where Adam and his grandfather were still standing, chatting about the latest happenings in town. An old shack outside of town had caught fire the other day, and it had taken quite the fight to put it out. His gramps had thought they should have let it burn to the ground. "It wasn't doing much good for anything anyway," his grandfather said, continuing on with their conversation as though Adam's father hadn't said a thing.

Adam tried to break free of the conversation in order to talk to his father, but just when his grandfather stopped talking, the back door was flung open and his younger brother plowed inside with bags in each hand.

"Hope I'm not too late," he said, shrugging out of his jacket before carrying the bags into the other room. "The damned truck stalled on the highway. Right outside of town."

"Language," their mother called out from an unknown location in the kitchen—a wall separated her and her sons.

"Why didn't you call one of us? We would've gone out and gotten ya," Gramps said, following Conner into the living room.

They all followed him through the house like he was the main attraction. Someone they hadn't seen in a while, almost as though a stranger had decided today was a good day to have supper with the family.

Adam leaned against the old oak doorframe of the living room, watching Conner unload his duffle bags, pulling out a change of clothes and whatever else he had stuffed in them. Covered in mud and grease, Conner held up a hand offering a high five as he walked past. Adam gave a half-assed attempt, turned and watched as Ava cried out for "Unle Onner," unable or just plain refusing to pronounce her c's as she held outstretched arms above her head and chased him around the living room. Without a care of the dirt and grease smudged across his face, she hugged him close, smearing his face against hers.

If there was anything that proved Ava was made for the country life, this was it. The girl didn't make a fuss about dirt. Hell, the kid loved to get dirty. That girl would play outside all day, every day, if she could.

Conner turned to Adam, smiling with the acceptance of love from Ava. "This girl's a keeper."

"Have you seen her mom?" Gramps said, nudging his darned elbow into Adam once again, the chuckle contagious throughout the room. "Wowza."

His grandfather had a good point. Ava had picked up quite a few characteristics from Rachel. Her blue eyes, blonde hair, and that silly smile of hers. Definitely something he looked forward to seeing every night after a long day of work.

"I heard that," Adam's grandmother called out, walking out behind Rachel with a heaping bowl of mashed potatoes. She set it on the pot holder on the table next to the gravy, before shaking a finger at Gramps from across the room. "You'll think wowza when you're sleeping alone tonight."

With that, the room dispersed, offering a quick sympathetic look at their grandfather. Ava was handed off to Adam before Conner ran off to shower.

"Time to eat," his mother called out from the dining room table as she dried her hands on her apron. Flopping a spoonful of requested potatoes on his father's plate, his mother smiled and passed the bowl around.

Unfolding the high chair, he slid it up to the table; he placed Ava between his and Rachel's spot at the table. He needed to go out and holler for Tyler, but before he had the chance, Rachel had already opened the front door and was summoning the boy inside. She had it all under control as she pointed to the spare bathroom, directing Tyler to wash up before coming to the table.

Her eyes caught his, sending arousal pressing against his pants. This woman had a helluva way of turning any situation into something more. Holy hell, it was hot in here. He fanned the collar of his shirt away from his neck.

The slight blush against her cheeks told him that she was feeling what he was. If there was a way to escape without the family noticing, he'd take care of their situation real quick-like, making sure she understood exactly what she did to him.

Tyler raced out of the bathroom, whizzed past Rachel, and grabbed a spot at the table between his grandparents. Ava slapped the table, turning Adam and Rachel's attention back to the here and now. She was ready to eat, evidenced by the way her fists balled up and her eyes focused on the bowl of mashed potatoes.

Pulling Rachel's chair out, he waited for her to be seated before sliding it up to the table and taking his own seat. Ava jabbered on while she kept her eyes on him as he scooped a spoonful of potatoes onto her plate.

Lifting a fork, preparing to stuff his face with the delicious food his mother cooked for them, Adam's bite was interrupted by his grandfather's question. "What's the plan for the fire department?"

Diverting his eyes from his father's heavy stare, Adam shrugged. He hadn't come today to talk about the fire department or politics, or anything that heavy. He wanted to enjoy the time they had together like they had for the last several family dinners.

As though on cue, Conner entered the dining room, playing a hand through his damp hair before finding a place to sit. "What'd I miss?"

Adam bit his tongue. The answer he wanted to give wasn't the answer his brother was looking for. Too much of it was too bitter for an answer, so Adam swallowed the words with a mouthful of lemonade.

The shift of tension spread throughout the dining room, surrounding them like a thick fog of unsettled words. His father's eyes told him that something was coming, something that was going to stir the pot and get everyone bickering. Adam hoped it wouldn't happen like that, but he knew his family, and the last thing to happen would be a calm, civilized conversation.

Rachel must have sensed it too, because the look of discomfort had crossed her face several times in the last several minutes. Why his family couldn't all get along was lost on him—or his father, he should say. The trouble had found them when Conner had announced his move to Colorado. His family couldn't accept it and move on. Instead, they had come to dwell on it, month after month, year after year.

"I heard that Megan O'Brien's thinking about joining the department," Gramps said, shortly after taking a bite of mashed potatoes. Adam loved that man, but he sure as heck didn't know how to take a hint.

Adam nodded, deciding not to continue ignoring his grandfather's questions. "She talked about it the other night at Levy's. She's coming in Monday to have a talk with me about it."

"She's always been one to solve a problem when she sees it," Gramps said, spooning another helping of potatoes onto his plate. "I'm sure Rosie's just tickled over the whole thing."

From the corner of his eye, he caught sight of Conner fidgeting, trying to stay low and out of the conversation. Adam wondered how close he and Megan actually were. That'd be saved for another discussion. He was sure there'd be plenty of time to discuss that—if and when the time was right, and it surely wasn't right now.

"She's not too happy about it," Rachel said, using the corner of her napkin to guard against her half eaten food. "She talked about it the other day at Granny Mae's."

"Do you think the department is going to hire her, Adam?" His grandfather's question was one of complete innocence. As if his grandfather just now caught the wave of tension radiating from Adam's father on his left, he shrugged and said, "Well, I only ask because I know how many hours you've been pulling to make ends meet around there. I'm sure Megan will be a fine addition to the squad."

"I don't think a girl could handle the job, Gramps," Conner said with that big, ol' dumb smirk of his.

A grunt sounded from the opposite end of the table. Adam knew exactly what was coming next. Jacobsen family war, round two. "You think you can do the job any better, boy?"

The added emphasis on the *boy* was a subtle indication of how upset their father actually was. He hadn't given up his care about the department since his retirement. Heck, if Adam had to say anything about that, he thought his father cared more now, than ever. Which had become obvious due to the heated arguments they'd had recently.

Conner shoveled food into his mouth as though it was going to be his last supper. Adam remembered the days of being young and dumb, carefree, but now those days were gone and soon would be for Conner, too.

"I could do a heck of a lot better than a girl," Conner mumbled, short of clarity and confidence as he looked down at his plate.

"I think you'd better give that another thought or two," their father said, clearing his spot at the table. The look his father gave Conner was one that would have done some harm if Conner wasn't self-absorbed. "Because the last time I checked, you ran..."

"I didn't run," Conner said, now looking their father straight in the eye. His cheeks red and his eyes burned with whatever hate he had for the man. "I took a better offer and made something of myself rather than..."

He cut himself off after taking a look at Adam and the surrounding family. Adam knew what he wanted to say. Cedar Valley hadn't offered him anything worth sticking around for. Adam wouldn't have stuck around either, if it hadn't been for the department.

The silence that hung around them was more awkward and painful than the tension had been. His grandfather grabbed for his napkin, causing his fork and knife to clatter against the plate, breaking the silence. "I'll tell you something," he said, frustration and anger twisted his face. "Back in my day, families didn't argue like this. Instead, they came together and did what's right. Put your pride aside, boy, and do what's right."

His words were directed straight at Conner, who was sitting with his arms crossed in front of him as he leaned forward on the table, and after a long minute, he said, "Hell, I've already done that."

Gramps called bullshit with his grunt and a shake of his head, but Conner corrected him by saying the next words no one thought they'd hear in a million years. "I'm here to stay."

18

"*H*ave you talked to Adam about Megan yet?"

Rosie's question was full of desperation, but Rachel had to be honest and up front with her. She had talked to Adam, and as far as she knew, Megan had a spot guaranteed on the squad. Not because Adam didn't take Rosie's wishes into consideration, but because Megan was needed and would make a great addition to the team—Adam's words, not hers. She barely knew Megan, except for the fact that she had been right there alongside Leah after the wreck, when she herself couldn't be.

"Rosie," Rachel said, taking hold of her hand and leading her into the back room filled with mixers and fresh ingredients for round number three of baking all day. Finding an empty spot along the counter, Rachel nestled herself right up there. "The department needs volunteers."

Rosie's eyes clouded with realization. Tears dared to

fall, but remained welled along the bottoms of Rosie's eyes. "I know that. I just..."

Reassurance was all Rachel could afford to give Rosie, something that she needed to hear. It wasn't a promise, because Rachel couldn't make promises that had no guarantee to be kept, but she knew that Adam would do his best to keep the whole team safe. He would do whatever it took to make sure everyone came home safe each and every night. "Megan will do just fine," she finally said, after struggling to find the right words. "She's a damned good paramedic, and I know she'll fit right in with the others on the squad. They all love her."

"I know they do," Rosie said, drying the tears that had escaped with the top of her apron. It pained Rachel to see Rosie so upset, but she knew that everything would be okay. The department needed volunteers. Adam needed volunteers. It would all work out. "It's just the thought of something happening to her. I..."

"From what I see and hear, there is no better team than the one we have here in the department," Rachel said, adding emphasis on no better team. She wasn't lying. She had never seen departments, all departments from law enforcement, medics, and fire, come together and love another like family. It was hard to find, and being from the city, she could vouch for Cedar Valley's willingness to reach out and support one another. That kind of thing didn't happen much in the city—not that she had any personal affiliation with them. You could tell a close knit service when you saw one. "She's in good hands."

Rachel looked forward to the day Adam wouldn't have to pull so many hours. He was getting overwhelmed with not being at home with her and the kids. He felt he was missing out on more than the average father, and it disappointed him. She could see it on his face every time she mentioned what Tyler and Ava had done together once home for the day. Normal conversations weren't normal anymore. They were becoming a slap in his face, and she couldn't help but wish for something to change.

"Thank you, Rach," Rosie said, dabbing the last of her tears from her cheeks as she looked in the mirror to make sure her makeup still looked good. "Sometimes these hormones get the best of me."

"It's okay, I know exactly how that is," she said, offering Rosie a hug. She had known hormones all too well during her pregnancy. There were several days when she couldn't control her emotions. She had been one giant mood swing, day after day.

Rosie shuffled through the swinging doors after offering Rachel a quick peck on the cheek. She remembered the first time meeting Rosie, how sweet and kindhearted the woman had been. Nothing had changed since then and Rachel was thankful for that.

The whirling mixer hummed as she gathered her next set of ingredients. Today, she would be making her favorite cupcakes, from scratch and extra sweet. She loved to imitate Betty Crocker's mix with a special recipe of her own. She especially enjoyed hearing the compliments and generous comparisons between hers and other cupcakes the customers had eaten before.

Today was cupcake day, which in fact, was also the day that a special order was to be made. This busy weekend ahead included her best friend, Leah, who was so far along she couldn't tie her own shoes anymore. She had long since switched to slip-ons and Velcro.

Rachel had tried so hard not to laugh the day they got together over chocolate shakes last week, but it was so hard not to, with the memory of how awful it was for Rachel when she had gotten to that stage of pregnancy. And that's not including getting up out of your seat, either.

After pouring the chocolatey mix into the liners, she placed the pans into the preheated oven and shut the door. She was more than excited to get started on the cupcakes for Leah's baby shower, but she needed to keep a decent amount of time between batches. She had learned that from the first day, when she had several cookies waiting to be frosted and hadn't even eaten lunch yet. Granny Mae had emphasized *Take your time and give yourself some time, too.*

As though she needed a subtle reminder, her stomach grumbled and growled, indicating it was time for a short break. Walking out front, the cafe was crowded with their regular customers. It seemed funny that the women in town gathered here while their husbands gathered for lunch at Levy's. Something about a man and his grilled food, they'd say.

"Rachel," an older woman called out from a table nearby. The woman was seated with a few other women Rachel recognized from the recent newspaper article— something about members of some sort of association dealing with cards and what not. She hadn't paid much attention to it, because Ava had demanded she play Barbies and baby dolls all day that day.

As Rachel neared the table, she reached for an empty chair and sat down. She had a few minutes before she needed to get the cupcakes out of the oven. Soon, the smell would drift out into the dining area and everyone would be requesting to know what was for dessert.

"Tell me, how's Cedar Valley treating you?" the older woman asked, taking a sip of her coffee, proper etiquette and all.

"Good," Rachel said with a smile. "I love it here. Everyone's so nice and welcoming. It's like we're one big family."

The whites of the women's dentures shined when they chuckled and offered agreement with what she had said. These women wore their lipstick bright and their mascara flawlessly. She would love to get makeup guidance from them if they'd offer. She chuckled at the thought of them offering out of pity. *Bless your heart, dear,* they would say as they gathered around with their tips and much needed advice.

She saw the look they all gave one another, as if something needed to be said, but no one wanted to say it or had the right words to use. Rachel shifted in her chair. The timer on the oven would ding any minute and the sudden silence at the table had her all sorts of uncomfortable. It was hard to know what these ladies were up to. Maybe they were mind readers and they were willing to offer her some much needed guidance after all. Rachel wouldn't turn it down. Motherhood had welcomed her with wide open arms to a world of messy hair, no time for hours in front of a mirror, and definitely no time to dress accordingly. She had found herself wearing yoga pants nine times out of ten—only dressing up once in a while, for family events for example. And by dressing up, she meant actually putting on a pair of jeans and a shirt that wasn't stained or well worn.

"What would you say if we asked you to bake for our annual event?" a woman sitting to the left of bright pink asked.

"Hold that thought," Rachel said, holding a finger up as she darted off toward the kitchen. She hoped she hadn't taken too long. The last thing she wanted was burnt cupcakes. The smell of chocolate surrounded her as she stumbled through the swinging door.

Throwing a mitt on, she hovered near the oven, peeking in at what could be a waste of four dozen cupcakes. They seemed to look okay. The main test would be to get them out and try one. The dinger had gone off a few minutes ago, but she knew how delicate those minutes were when it came to baking—the time between moist and burnt—critical condition.

Pulling them out, she placed them on a rack to cool. She would have to try one after a bit. Right now, she wanted to get back out and talk with these ladies about this annual event of theirs.

THE ANNUAL BAKE off was this weekend. The ladies were desperate to win the grand prize—$10,000. They wouldn't tell Rachel what the money would go towards, but she couldn't turn them down.

She penciled in her schedule of baking, making the annual event second to Leah's cupcakes. The baby shower was Saturday. The event was Sunday—something Rachel may have heard about, but like everything else lately, it took a place on the back burner.

The event was to include everyone from miles around.

A fair rule mentioned was for all baking to be done by scratch. The women had mentioned there would be no problem for Rachel.

As though the mixer understood the constraint of her to-do list, it sputtered flour in heaps onto the cupboards and countertop. Another mess for Rachel to clean up, but it would have to wait until the last of the cupcakes were out of the oven. She hated leaving messes until later. She had picked up the trait from her grandmother, who seldom left a mess until the very end of a job. There was no way around it when she had spent most of her time with her grandmother. But, there was always a first for everything. Like leaving a mess and entering a bunch of cupcakes into a town's annual bake off that was less than a few days away and the clock was ticking.

She sent multiple texts to Adam, requesting to know what she had gotten herself into, and had sent the same text messages to Leah demanding answers.

Leah's answers were a lot different than Adams. Where Adam had told her that she had gotten herself into it, she was a good baker and people knew it. He had mentioned something along the lines of *can't hide from natural talent when you've got it.* Leah had answered with as much sarcasm as she could with a straight *but you love me.*

It was true, she loved Leah, and loved the town, too. The two combined gave her business and offered her a chance to spread her amazing sweetness around—which now sounded dirtier than her mixer was at the moment.

Sending a text back to Adam, she told him that she would be pulling longer hours at the cafe now, and could possibly swing having Ava and Tyler in the back with her. That way, she wouldn't have to keep Ava long at daycare and Tyler could help out. He loved baking as much as he loved football, and she couldn't deny how much his passion for baking could help her right now.

She would pick the kids up in a couple of hours. It was a done deal. Supper wouldn't be on the table when Adam got home, which he said was perfectly all right. He'd stop by Levy's when he got off and order pizza for them when she gave word of heading home.

She finished up with the last of the buttercream frosting for the ten dozen cupcakes she had made for the cafe. She would come in early the next day to set them out in the display case next to the register. It had taken less time than she had thought, but it was now nearing three p.m. and she had kids to pick up.

Wiping her hands on her apron, she finished cleaning up the mess she had left throughout the mixing and the baking of these cupcakes. Setting aside the containers, she wiped down the countertops and cupboards the best she could.

They'd be coming right back to start on Leah's baby shower cupcakes as soon as she picked up Ty and Ava. Little did they know about the last minute surprise. She hoped Tyler would be as excited as she was, if not more. Ava would be a breeze, because not only did she like to get dirty, she loved to help her momma bake, too—or at least that's what Rachel made her believe she was doing.

"I'll be back in less than twenty," she called out to Rosie and Granny Mae as she hung her apron on the hook by the back door. Grabbing her keys, she headed out into the sunshine that had been absent the last few days. She had enjoyed the thunderstorms, but two days of storms was too many without the sun.

The warm rays pelted against her face as she unlocked her car and opened the door. Just as she was sliding into the driver's seat, sirens blared as firetrucks zoomed by, heading east toward the highway.

Pulling out of the parking lot, she fought the urge to follow the line of trucks. It wasn't the fact her boyfriend was on one of them, but the sight of the heavy smoke coming from the area just north of the highway.

19

*A*dam had hustled out of the office and into the truck when the tones dropped. A field fire had gotten out of control, dispatch relayed over the paging system. Some farmer must have been burning ditches, but hadn't gotten the message that there was a burn ban here and the surrounding areas. *Damn.*

Climbing into the truck, he was met by a smiling face, eager for her first actual fire call. "Welcome to your first fire."

"Thanks," Megan said, offering him a high five with her free hand as she struggled with the buckle. It was obvious that her adrenaline was amped, but just about everyone's would be when the tones dropped, unless of course, they were seasoned fighters and had been there and done that for the majority of these calls.

Crackling over the truck's radio, dispatch notified them that the fire was now covering the majority of the field and engulfing a nearby barn. Upping the priority to urgent, dispatch also notified responding units that the barn contained thousands of pounds of farm chemicals.

Adam knew the possibility of an explosion was high once the fire managed to take over that barn. Ammonium nitrate, along with other chemicals in fertilizer, once met with an open flame, can cause a violent explosion.

Flying past Granny Mae's cafe, he hoped that Rachel hadn't heard wind of this fire. He didn't want her to worry more than she already did. His main focus, with or without an explosion, was to get this call under control and everyone go home safe.

Heading east on the highway, it was more than evident where the fire was. The north side of the highway was a dirty shade of gray mixed with a tarnished yellow haze. Providing more evidence that this was a bad situation, dispatch notified that Hazmat was less than five miles out, and the farmer was refusing to stand back. What the hell? The perfect ingredients for an out of control fire, all they needed was someone to throw some farm animals into the mix.

"Deputies on scene have advised the barn is fully engulfed," dispatch yelled into the radio, adrenaline apparent through their voice. They were less than two minutes from scene and Adam could see the ugliness rearing to life.

RACHEL TRIED to focus on getting the kids and heading back to the cafe, but she couldn't take her attention away from the smoke that now clouded the whole town with an acrid smell that burnt.

No one she talked to had any idea of what was happening; all they knew was deputies had blocked off five miles east and west of the fire's location.

Rachel prayed for the safety of all involved, including Adam. He had just told her this morning that it was Megan's second day on the job and she was doing fantastic. The thought of this being her first and only fire...

"Kids, get inside," she said, guiding them towards the backdoor of Granny Mae's. Walking in, the café was buzzing with conversation and worry. The television aired with video from a helicopter's live recording. Apparently, a farmer was burning ditches and the flames were out of control.

Diverting the kids' attention from the commotion, she brought them closer to the back of the baking area. Tyler was old enough to know when a situation wasn't right, and the look on his face told her so. Ava found her own distraction with a makeshift drum set involving pots and pans and a wooden spoon. Tyler, on the other hand, looked at Rachel for explanation. His father, the love of her life, was fighting this raging fire—against the odds of an explosion.

"Hon, he's good at what he does," she said, mustering up enough conviction to shadow her own doubts of how ugly this could get. "He's got one heck of a team out there with him. They'll get this taken care of in no time at all."

She tousled a hand through the boy's damp hair—an effect of the sweltering heat, along with the news of his father fighting this fire. Feeling horrible, but wanting to keep his mind on other things, she offered him the chance to make the first batch by himself—a temporary distraction.

Watching Tyler read through the recipe, gather the ingredients, and mix them together like a pro, she couldn't help but smile. He was so passionate with baking, making sure he didn't miss anything as he stirred it all into the mixer prior to turning it on.

Ava had entertained herself well enough over the last hour with the pots and pans, which were now scattered about the floor, covering the back half of the unused space. Rachel knew it was better to leave her be, because she had her hands full as it was with keeping Tyler distracted and staying on track with the requests of all these cupcakes for the coming events of this weekend.

The thought of what would happen if something went awry with the fire, if something happened to Adam, or Megan, or any one of them out there fighting this raging beast...

There was no sense in thinking the worst, but it was something she couldn't help doing. She reached for the clean mixer sitting on the counter next to Tyler's area. Gathering the ingredients for her much loved buttercream frosting, she decided to mix it now so they'd have it once the cupcakes in the oven were done and cool enough to frost. Besides, she needed to busy herself to take her mind off of what may be the worst day of their lives.

HOLLERING OUT OVER THE RADIO, Adam maintained calm throughout his squad. They needed to stay calm and focused. Something that was easier said than done with their first fire of the year, along with the largest and most violent fire to date.

Cedar Valley seldom faced the threat of explosions. In all of the years he had lived here, and even the years before his parents moved here, fires like this hadn't happened.

Directing a new line of attack on this fire, he managed to form a strategic line of fighters along the front and side of the barn. So far, they were managing to keep the flames away from the chemicals stored inside. The farmer swore he hadn't heard there was a burn ban, and he thought since there was plenty of rain the last few days, it was safe enough for a fire.

Adam had to bite his tongue on a few choice words as he went on with his job, directing the farmer to stand back, as he motioned toward the deputies who were controlling the crowd of onlookers. People were out of their minds to be standing around, dismissing the fact that this fire could easily cause an explosion that could wipe them out.

The crowd that had formed was slowly being cleared out, but not fast enough. Hell, if he had a choice, he wouldn't be anywhere near this place. Hazmat had given him a rundown of what could possibly happen, but it didn't take a rocket scientist to figure that out. The whole thing had a high probability of going boom and taking out everyone within a hundred yards.

He needed to notify dispatch that they needed additional resources—to send additional help from surrounding counties. This fire wasn't settling for anything less than what they had to offer—their lives included. He had no choice but to push pride aside and radio for more help. This fire was going to take more man power than what they had—especially if everyone was going home safe tonight.

Just when the radio clicked, he witnessed the biggest explosion he'd ever seen in his entire life, right before the feeling of being thrown the length of a football field and everything going black.

20

The news of the explosion was all over the news. It was being broadcast that the explosion occurred shortly after the request for more manpower. The local firefighters had radioed shortly before the explosion that the fire was too large for them to beat by themselves. Surrounding counties had been paged and were en route two minutes after the notification. There was no update on the condition of those involved in the blast—all they knew was that it was bad, and the prognosis looked devastating.

No sooner than the news aired, Rosie panicked. Swearing she should have stood her ground and never let Megan volunteer. Rachel empathized where Rosie was concerned, but at the same time, Megan would've been there regardless the situation. The ambulance was staged not too far from the blast, and as far as Rachel could tell, the medics had been too close to the explosion, too.

Everyone was on edge, waiting for the next update, while trying to contact those involved. Rachel had heard a few of the women huddled close to the counter mention that Cedar Valley had never experienced such a catastrophe. She had heard enough when they began talking about fatalities. She wasn't ready to hear it.

Walking into the backroom, she found Tyler right where he had been when she took a breath of not so fresh air. Ava had moved on to bigger and better things, like banging on the front of the oversized, industrial refrigerator with a metal spoon. Rachel yearned for silence—she needed it now more than ever. The whole café was buzzing with the news and nerves were frayed just thinking about the worst.

Grabbing the spoon from Ava and quickly swapping it with a plastic spatula in time to avert the breakdown, Rachel allowed her to go back to what she had been doing —this time, much more quietly.

Her phone vibrated against the inside of her pocket and her stomach flipped. The thought of Adam texting her to let her know he was okay crossed her mind as she frantically pulled it from her denim capris. Trying to stabilize her emotions as she read the text from Leah, she took a few deep breaths.

I just saw everything on the news. What can I do?

As badly as she wanted to, Rachel couldn't let her emotions take over. She wanted to crawl into a corner of the room and cry from the agonizing thoughts of losing Adam. Instead, she had to be strong, not just for Adam, but for the kids, too. They, especially Tyler because Ava was too little to understand, didn't need to panic.

Tyler continued with the last batch of cupcake mix. He had done well in the last few hours. It was nearing six o'clock. This is the time Adam should have been relieved from his shift and heading to Levy's. Instead, he was...

I have no idea, Lee. I don't know what's going on or anything. I haven't heard anything.

Clicking send on her last message, she felt the weight of panic engulf her as she struggled to concentrate on what mattered most. No news was good news, or at least that's how the saying went, anyway.

Turning toward the kids, she asked if they'd like to go home. She was ready to call it a night here, knowing well enough the night wouldn't end soon enough. This nightmare of not knowing could possibly linger on for the next two hours.

Tyler's cupcake mix was poured into a separate bowl, covered and placed into the fridge that Ava had continuously beat on for the last half an hour. The girl never wavered from that activity, obviously enjoying the musical beat she had created.

Once buckled into the car and on their way home, she could tell Tyler was struggling with the news of the explosion. His gaze was fixed on the east side of town, where the once gray-colored skies had been mixed with a hazy yellow, and were now a lighter shade of smoke gray. She hated that they hadn't heard from anyone yet with the condition of the responding units, those who had been on scene when the explosion occurred. She would have loved to have an update, like yesterday, so she'd know what to tell the kids.

"Hey, bud," she said, gently reaching out for his arm to grab his attention from the direction of the unknown. If she hadn't known any better, she would have headed in that direction, pulled Adam out of the crowd, and begged him to walk away from the department before it cost him his life. Heaviness inside her prayed that it wasn't too late.

Pulling into the driveway minutes after leaving the café, she rounded the kids out of the car and herded them into the house. Not wanting Ava to get absorbed and wreak havoc with her toys, she put her favorite movie into the DVD player—Frozen, for the umpteenth time that week, and Ava couldn't have cared less how many times she had watched it.

Tyler followed her into the dining room, where they both pulled out chairs and sat down. It was hard to find words to say when the words weren't there.

Instead of struggling through a choice of words, she took hold of his hands, told him everything was going to be okay.

"How do you know?" he asked. His question was innocent, without accusation or attitude, but it pierced through her nonetheless. Ten years old, having already lost his mother, and now worried he was going to lose his father, too.

"Ty," she said, choking back the emotion that threatened to escape along the lines of her trembling lips. "I don't, but we've got to have faith that everything's okay. That your dad and everyone else involved is okay."

She watched him bow his head over his folded hands. And as he said a prayer for his father to make it home, she begged God for there to be a happy ending to this horrible nightmare, which had shadowed its evilness into their lives.

I_T WASN'T TOO MUCH LATER_ that she received the news she had been dreading to hear. No news certainly wasn't good news, as far as Cedar Valley was concerned. The explosion had wiped out a good portion of the response team, along with taking everything the surrounding counties had to offer, in order to take care of the injured.

She still wasn't sure if Adam was among those who were injured, and she had certainly prayed and begged enough in the last hour, to barter with the Lord himself if push came to shove.

Leah's text messages hadn't ended. She had continuously made sure Rachel and the kids were doing okay as they waited out the never ending battle of not knowing. She had even offered to come over and sit with them if it would ease Rachel's troubled mind. Rachel couldn't say no. If there was any time when she needed her best friend, this was it. Even if that best friend wanted to share a pint of Ben and Jerry's ice cream, she wouldn't refuse that either. Except right now, nothing sounded good as her stomach flopped at the thought of Adam being all alone in a hospital bed because word hadn't gotten to his family yet.

The knock at the door startled her. She had just tucked Ava into bed a few minutes ago, and though she had insisted that Leah really didn't need to come over, that she'd be fine, she opened the door to an overly swollen pregnant best friend and her husband.

Bringing each of them into her arms, she couldn't thank them enough for coming over. Tyler had been sitting on the couch, his eyes glued to the television when the news came on to give them an update.

"I've messaged him and called surrounding hospitals,"

Rachel told them, out of earshot of Tyler. "They're swamped with patients, but can't tell me if they have Adam, or anyone for that matter."

The news reporter verified that it remained unclear how many were injured, but the fatalities were still at zero. Thankful for that, Rachel kept her attention on the update. The reporter couldn't give any more information as far as who had been injured on scene, but would relay that information as soon as she knew. The camera scanned over what was left from the explosion. The skeletal remains of an old car, the metal frame of what she figured was some sort of farming equipment, and a few other things she wasn't even sure what they could have been.

The cause of the explosion was still under investigation, but there was a likelihood that it was caused when the flames came in contact with the fertilizers and other chemicals stored in the barn.

Rachel's thoughts scattered to Adam's family. She hadn't thought once about calling them. Looking at Leah and Liam, she asked if she could make a phone call, if they were all right with keeping an eye on Tyler, who had dozed off on his end of the couch, under a Teenage Mutant Ninja Turtles blanket—something that would shield what was left of his youth.

Grabbing her phone off the kitchen table, she walked through the sliding doors and onto the back porch. The night was an eerie calm, with a sky full of brightly shining stars. The moon cast its presence just east of the peak of the house.

Feeling guilty for not thinking to call his parents earlier, she kept her emotions in check as she waited for them to answer. By the third ring, she was about to hang up until Adam's mother answered on the other end.

Rachel asked if they had heard anything yet, and much like her and everyone else, they hadn't. They were hoping for the best of course, but they weren't allowed near the scene—Adam's father had already tried once in an attempt to find Adam.

Irrational thoughts came to Rachel's mind as she listened to another mother weep over the possible injury or loss of her son. She couldn't bear to hear it, so she told her she would call if she heard from him and they would do the same.

Ending the conversation, Rachel inhaled a deep breath. Times like these were few and far between, and something she had never experienced before. She had never before fallen in love with a firefighter, or really, anyone who risked their lives for others. Scott had been far from that category with his construction business.

Scott...The letter she had received in the mail from his attorney had seemed to be the end of the world, and had caused so much stress. If only she had known that it wasn't even close to the nightmare she was in now, she wouldn't have batted an eye.

Taking yet another deep breath, she released it slowly before sliding the door open. Closing it behind her, she couldn't help the feeling of helplessness.

"The news just said they have an update from the deputies who were on scene," Leah said, motioning for Rachel to come sit down next to her. "The deputies said that there were three firefighters taken to St. Mary's in Rockford."

Rachel's thoughts swarmed with the realization that

Adam could be among those taken in for treatment. She knew the hospital wouldn't tell her over the phone, so she needed to go there. Where ever Adam may be, she needed to find him and let him know that she was there.

Leah insisted that Liam drive her. They had both insisted she was in no condition to drive herself. Leah also insisted that she would stay at the house with the kids, and to let her know as soon as Rachel found out.

Rachel kissed Ava's forehead, tucking the blankets under her for extra security through the night and when she made her way to the living room again, she whispered into Tyler's ear that she was going to find his father, and that everything was going to be all right. Choking back the emotion for the thousandth time that night, Rachel hugged Leah and followed Liam out to his truck, which was parked less than twenty steps from the front porch.

He opened the door and assisted her in stepping inside before closing the door once she was seated. Rachel watched him walk around the front of the truck, wave to Leah who was standing in the doorway, and climb into the cab.

The truck grumbled to life with a turn of the key and for the majority of the ride to the hospital, the rev of the engine was the only sound she heard.

21

The beeping of the machines echoed noisily by his head. The hum of the blood pressure cuff on his arm and the squeak of the IV pump was irritating. He wanted nothing more than to get out of here.

The nurse had insisted he stay, allowing them to monitor him over night. He must have been knocked out by the pain meds they shot through him, because he hadn't remembered any more conversation about it.

He had thought he was mistaken, or possibly dreaming, when Rachel pushed back the curtain to his room and walked in. He definitely could have been mistaken with all of the meds flowing through his bloodstream.

She raised a hand to cover her face, but he could still see the tremble of her lips and the tears as they fell, shadowing her cheeks on their way down.

He tried to raise his hand to motion her to come over to him, but his hands felt like they were tied to a ton of bricks. Another side effect of the meds, he imagined.

Liam came into the room once Rachel took another

step forward. Adam couldn't see too well in the darkened room, but he knew it was Liam by his stance and the buzzed haircut—an incident unspoken of that had to do with Leah and her first attempt at cutting his hair with trimming shears. All Adam knew was that it had ended with a visit to the local barber, who had to fix it.

Adam tried to talk, but the dry, scratchy feeling in his throat, like he had been sitting around a campfire inhaling all the smoke, was overwhelming.

Pain etched across Rachel's face as she neared the bed, reaching for him through the rails along the side. Tears flooded her eyes, causing her makeup to stain her cheeks. She still looked beautiful.

He tried once again to tell her he was okay, but was stopped short by the same feeling he had a minute ago. He knew where he was, and he knew where he had been prior to being here, but he couldn't remember what had happened between then and now.

"I'm sorry," Rachel choked on the words as she turned away. There was another failed attempt on his part to reach out for her with arms that felt like bricks.

A nurse was heard entering the room, and in that exact minute, he heard the words explosion and smoke inhalation. The injuries hadn't taken his life, that was obvious... The explosion had caused some major injuries that would heal with time. What injuries the nurse was talking about he wasn't sure of, because no matter how hard he tried to sit up in order to get a good look, he couldn't. He was stuck in this supine position and his only view was of the ceiling and the monitors in his peripheral.

"The injuries you see will heal with time," the nurse said, her voice low and calm. "But the internal injuries, both physical and possibly psychological, may take some extra time to overcome."

"What kind of internal injuries are there?" Rachel asked, her voice full of concern.

He so badly wanted to tell her that he was okay. That everything was going to be okay. He was going to be released soon and everything would be back to normal.

"Aside from his broken arm and bruised ribs, which we assume he got from being tossed in the explosion," the nurse said, speaking low enough for Adam to not hear, but he heard every word. "He experienced smoke inhalation and a minor concussion."

There was a long pause before the nurse said, "We expect him to be released within the next few days, as long as his oxygen stats stay above ninety-five and his pain level is managed well with the medicines."

He could hear Rachel's sigh from across the room. "Can we talk to him?"

The pain in Rachel's voice was evident. The way she sounded was the way he felt. Consumed by the ugly reality of what really happened, he wondered if she'd ever let him go back to fighting fires. If he had to guess, the answer would be no. Point blank. He couldn't, nor would he, blame her.

Then it hit him, the thought of those who were around him on scene. Were they all right? How would he find out?

The explosion must have happened when he had least expected it. The only memory he had was radioing dispatch to request more trucks. They were being over-powered by the flames and the possibility had reached its high for not being able to keep the flames back much longer than they had.

It was Megan's first fire. He had promised Wes and Rosie, and Megan... hell, his whole crew, that he would keep them from danger. He had called the shots and now there was a possibility that they were injured...or worse.

His last thought had been cursing the farmer for not thinking things through, before consciousness eluded him once again.

WORD HAD TRAVELED QUICKLY about the hospitalization of Adam and a few of his crew members, including Megan, whose only injury was a stitch-able fix. She had been hit with flying debris while being thrown by the blast. The nurses and doctors had told the family and friends who were crowded into the small, musty smelling waiting area that their prognosis looked good. None of them had experienced severe life threatening injuries, aside from Adam's smoke inhalation, which had threatened to inflame his airway, but someone had rushed to his side and intubated him within minutes after the explosion.

No one had any idea who it was that saved Adam, and they probably never would. As it was explained by another fireman, when a scene becomes that hectic, it's enough just to know that someone is being taken care of —no one is worried about who is taking care of whom, unless it's you being taken care of and vice versa.

His words had been blunt, but they were the reality of the whole situation. The flames had raged out of control and everything else had escalated quickly. No one knows what exactly happened in the minutes of chaos. All they knew was there was an explosion and they were lucky there were no fatalities.

That's all that mattered to all of them. Everyone made it out alive.

IT TOOK days for Adam's release from the hospital, but once he was cleared, he was more than ready to get home. Rachel had driven back and forth from the hospital numerous times, leaving the kids with Leah as needed, but on the last day, they had decided it was more than okay for the kids to come with her.

Tyler's arms were wrapped tightly around Adam's neck as soon as they entered the room. He couldn't do much with a broken arm, as far as hugging went, but he had his voice back. "Hi, bud," he said, his words pressed against the side of his son's cheek. Tyler's body shook as emotion escaped, causing them both to shake. He could only comfort his son the best way he knew how. "Hey, don't cry, I'm okay. I'm here, bud. Everything's going to be okay."

Ava clung to Rachel, giving him an unsure look. It reminded him of her first time with Santa at the fire department. She had been scared to death of that guy, and hadn't wanted anything to do with him. She had the same look now, as though she was debating on running away or hiding, but at the same time, he could tell she was trying to figure it all out.

"Ava," he said, speaking soft in an attempt to let her know it was okay, it was still him she was looking at. It was the bulky casts on his arms that had her so confused. He didn't blame her. "Hey, hon, it's me."

Her face wrinkled with confusion. Her nose crinkled and with squinted eyes, she said, "Dadda?"

"Yes, honey, it's me," he said, doing his best to keep his emotions in check. No one wanted to see a grown man cry. And he certainly didn't want to, not when he couldn't wipe his own face.

Rachel put Ava down and no sooner had her feet hit the floor, than she was running in his direction with her arms spread wide and a pouty face only a father could love.

She climbed onto his lap with the assistance of her mother, pushing aside Tyler as she nestled close to his chest. Tyler shifted in his lap, making room for Ava.

Rachel sat next to him, placing a hand on his arm, she said, "I'm so glad you're okay. I wouldn't have known what to do otherwise."

Her words hit him hard. There was no guarantee that there would be a next time, but he did know that he didn't want to put her through what she had just gone through in the last seventy-two hours. It pained him to know she had just gone through what he had gone through with the death of Tyler's mother.

he weekend plans had been postponed to a later date. There was no baby shower and there certainly was not a bake off event in the nearby town park.

Leah had insisted that the baby shower be put off for a couple of weeks, allowing the time it would take to get things back to as normal as humanly possible.

The cupcakes for both events were stacked neatly in the café's freezer, waiting to be thawed out when the time was right. Which, according to the ladies who had become regular fans of Rachel's baking, the annual bake off would be the following weekend, as long as things were still improving as far as the injured were concerned. They had announced to Rachel that the grand prize, if won, would go to the Cedar Valley Fire Department to assist with medical bills and new equipment. They knew that the prize was only ten thousand dollars, which is why they offered to put their own money, along with donations currently being collected around town, to make sure everything was well taken care of.

The mention of the owners of Rockford's diner, the one she and Leah had once worked at, brought tears to her eyes. They had donated well over twenty thousand to go towards the expenses wherever it was seen fit, with a promissory note to donate more if needed.

She would be forever in their debt for their kindness. They had always been there for her and Leah. Recently, last summer, they had given Leah a check to help out with the Spencer's bar when it had caught fire due to an unforeseen situation with Leah's ex.

She promised the ladies that the cupcakes were already made for the event. "They're in the freezer and will taste just as good and fresh once they thaw in time for the event."

The ladies left no sooner than they had come in, taking their designer bags and coffees with them. Rachel had to admit that they certainly weren't who she first judged them to be. Remembering the first day she had met them, with their designer bags, jewelry and well done makeup, she was more than certain they were the prissy type. But, as with all other things, Rachel had learned not to judge someone based on first impressions. She was definitely proved wrong when she did.

"Hey Rosie," she called out toward the counter, as she turned with the ladies dirty dishes. "How's Megan doing?"

Rosie had vented to Rachel a few days after the release from the hospital. Everyone had been sent home, and all were on the mend. Adam was getting better by the day and Rachel couldn't be more thankful for that. Rosie, on the other hand, was still quite upset that Megan had joined the squad, and even more upset that people she cared about had gotten badly hurt.

"She's been better," Rosie said, taking the dishes from Rachel and walking into the back room with her. She placed them in the basin of the sink and turned to face Rachel.

Rachel had seen this look on Rosie before, more than once, actually. A look of bewilderment, as if she was trying to find the right words to say without offending anyone.

"What's the matter, Rose?"

She was near to tears with quivering lips and the whole shebang. Rachel wrapped an arm around her shoulders, pulling her close to allow her to let loose of all the pent up emotion she had obviously been carrying around with her for days now.

Rosie's body shook against Rachel's as tears streamed freely, soaking into the fabric of Rachel's apron. "I'm sorry," Rosie said, swiping at her fallen tears, trying her best to regain composure. "I just... it's been a helluva week."

"You can say that again," Rachel said, assuring Rosie that she wasn't the only one with that opinion. The explosion had taken a toll on everyone, not just those who were injured, but the whole community. Cedar Valley was still in shock that something so careless had happened. The farmer had donated quite a bit of his own money to the donation pot—maybe to save face and insults, but people still wondered if he had his head on straight. "I'm just glad everyone's okay."

"Me, too, dear," Rosie said, wiping away the remaining tears that had soaked her skin. "Don't get me wrong, I'm so thankful no one was killed in that mess, but the thought they could have been..."

Rachel knew firsthand what it was like worrying about someone you love. She'd done it her whole life. First her mother, who many had thought led a perfect life, was a heroin addict for years. It had taken several medical interventions and the help of the courts to get her turned around. Rachel had worried endlessly, day and night, whether her mother was dead in the streets, without anyone by her side. Her father had been an average man, working in a local factory trying to make ends meet. Even though he promised Rachel he hadn't stopped caring for her mother, she knew he had. It had taken years, more than five, for her mother to overcome the addiction. That still didn't stop her father from filing for divorce and moving on with his life. Rachel couldn't stand the thought of all those empty promises he had spoken of...

"Has Adam talked to you about the incident?" Rosie asked, scooping a spoonful of ice cream from the carton and eating it. Rachel grabbed a spoon and helped herself, shoving a heaping amount into her mouth before nodding. "What'd he say about it? Does he remember anything?"

The other night he had talked with her about it. He could only remember bits and pieces, and some she knew he would, hopefully, never remember. "He remembers radioing dispatch for more manpower, but everything after that, he doesn't remember," she said, stealing one more spoonful of ice cream before Rosie put the lid on it and put it away. "Which is probably a good thing."

"Definitely so," Rosie said, using a sharpie marker to

write *Rosie's* on the lid before shoving the carton in the back of the freezer. "Megan remembers it all."

Rachel's eyes widened and her mouth dropped open. Poor Megan had to witness the whole thing, and knowing it was her first fire...

"She's doing okay with it," Rosie assured, giving a subtle shrug as if to dismiss the emotion that was creeping up again. "She got lucky in the aspect of injuries, but what she saw will haunt her for a while."

Rachel couldn't imagine what responders saw day after day, let alone an explosion. She knew she wouldn't have been able to do what they had. Nope, not at all. It took someone with a caring heart and gratitude for the community in order to put their life on the line...

"She's the one who intubated Adam," Rosie said, just throwing the words out like she had no idea what that little detail meant.

Rachel swallowed hard, with the thought of owing Megan so much more than a thank you. She wanted to hug that woman and worship the ground she walked on. This... was the reason that woman was the talk of the town when it came to being a badass... because she was. She had shoved her own injury aside to deal with those of others.

"She saved Adam's life," Rachel said, thinking of what it would have meant for Adam if Megan hadn't been there. "The nurse even said that if the person who intubated him hadn't been on scene, he would have..."

She couldn't finish the sentence. Death had come so close to their lives yet again, and she couldn't think of the loss Tyler would have experienced. Thank God that wasn't happening.

Rosie nodded in agreement with what Rachel had said. "No matter how many times I begged that girl not to go chasing fires," Rosie said, mumbling something else incoherent under her breath. "She saw Adam and one other get tossed from the blast. She saw the crowd gather around Adam, who wasn't moving. I don't know all the details, because she said she just went Paramedic mode and jumped into action."

"Thank God," Rachel whispered, more than thankful for Megan's efforts. That girl deserved a damned award.

Rosie smiled at the thought of her granddaughter saving someone's life, something she did every day, but that day it was more than just something she did... It was something she had to do, in spite of her own injuries.

"We've been trying to figure out who it was that saved his life," Rachel said, not wanting to dwell too long on the subject, but she wanted Rosie to know that because Megan was right there with the squad, she was able to do what needed to be done. She was a hero.

With a nod, Rosie motioned toward the swinging door and said, "I'd better get back to work. Are you going to put some goodies in the case out there?"

"Of course," Rachel said, grabbing the premade tray of cookies and bars she had made the other day, after Adam convinced her he was more than okay at home by himself. "Then I have to run somewhere, but I'll be back after lunch."

Placing the goodies into the display case next to the register, Rachel tossed the empty tray into the basin of the sink and grabbed her keys. She had a whole day of baking scheduled, but first, she needed to thank the one who saved the love of her life.

THANKING MEGAN HAD BEEN A CHALLENGE. Rachel found her words traveling in one ear and out the other, as Megan countered with an explanation that she was only doing what she was trained to do, nothing more than that.

Her explanation hadn't stopped Rachel from telling her how thankful she was, regardless if it was just her job or not. If it hadn't been for Megan and her ability to shift gears, Adam might not be here today to recount the horrible details of the blast, which he seemed to remember more bits and pieces of day after day of recovery.

23

*H*aving time off offered Adam a new perspective to the extra hours he had been putting in the last few months. That money was coming in handy now, since he'd be off on doctor's orders for at least a few more weeks, or until his injuries were healed and the doctor declared him ready to go back to work.

If he were honest, he enjoyed being home during the day with the kids, but he was more than ready to get back to the department. There was nothing more torturing than hearing the tones drop and being unable to go out and chase that adrenaline-filled call.

The knock at the door interrupted his reminiscing of what he was missing each day he wasn't on the trucks. Standing, taking a second or two to get his balance, he scooted toys out of his way as he made a path to the front door.

Giving the door a slight tug against the resistance of the door jam, Adam opened the door to a man identical to that of his brother, standing on his porch with bags at his feet. More than surprised when he realized that it was, in fact, his brother, he pulled Conner in for a half-assed hug as he wrapped his uninjured arm around the broad shoulders of his brother.

"What are you doing here?" His question was more of concern and surprise than one requesting an answer. "I thought you'd still be in Colorado."

Conner tossed his hands away from his sides, offering a subtle shrug before looking down at his packed bags. "I told y'all I was coming back, so... here I am," he said, offering Adam a smirk as he shoved his sunglasses to the top of his head.

Shoving the door, Adam held it open with his casted arm, allowing his brother time to gather the bags at his feet before stepping into the entryway. "Did you stop and see Mom and Dad yet?"

Dropping his bags on the bench of the banister rail, Conner shook his head. "I just drove straight here. I wanted to make sure you were doing okay, before I ventured around town."

Adam cleared another section of Ava's toys away from the front of the couch, including some of her favorite blocks, which she had stuffed inside the cushions. "Have a seat? Do you want anything to drink?"

Conner shrugged before taking a seat. "Nah, I'm good. Besides, I know where your fridge is."

Adam grabbed what he could of Ava's toys and tossed them into the bin next to the dining room. They would eventually take over the entire downstairs if he allowed it —which he had, until the night he stepped on a damned lego, then it was a whole different situation. Plus, there was no better time than now, while she was taking her afternoon nap, to clear the war zone of toys.

"Yeah, go ahead and help yourself," Adam motioned to the kitchen. "There's some leftover pizza from the other night, too."

It hadn't taken Conner a second time to hear the offer. He was up and headed for the kitchen in record time—less than two seconds.

"The plates are in..." Adam called out, stopping mid-sentence once he heard the rattle of dishes and the microwave humming to life.

Adam tossed the last of the toys into the bin just as Conner returned to the living room with a heaping pile of pizza on his plate. He sat down in the recliner and kicked his feet up, making himself right at home.

"What the hell? Did they not have any places to eat along the way?"

Conner absentmindedly took several more bites of food, followed up with a few quick swigs of beer. "Didn't take time to stop at any of them. I filled up both tanks in the truck, packed a cooler of water, and headed out."

Conner had obviously fared well with the thirteen hour trip. The man was just hungry and needing a beer, or two—all that was left in the fridge.

Placing his plate in the dishwasher, Conner came back to his spot, offering Adam a bottle of water. "You come here and drink all my beer, but I get offered a bottle of water?"

Shrugging, Conner kicked back in the recliner, getting comfortable before saying, "It isn't my fault you only had two beers in the fridge. Learn how to stock up."

Adam offered a smug grin in his brother's direction. "So, what's your plan of action here?"

Conner must have known the talk was coming because he had prepared himself by putting the recliner down, sat forward, and was now resting his elbows on his knees. "I actually stopped here first to check on you and ask about a position at the department."

Adam rested his casted arm along the arm of the couch, propped up with a pillow. He had been looking forward to having this conversation with his brother. Unfortunately, it had taken him getting hurt in order for Conner to come back home. It was more of a jagged, double-edged sword, but Adam would take it.

"You know it's yours as long as you want it," he said, giving Conner a look that begged him to say he wasn't joking. The department needed help, more now than ever with yet another few men short from injuries sustained during the job. Damned blast, anyway. It shouldn't have happened the way it had. They should have planned better for that situation. Shrugging off the conversation with himself, Adam figured *better luck next time*, hoping to hell there wouldn't ever be a next time, but knowing quite well the chance was always there, lurking in the shadows of every call. They never knew for sure what they were getting themselves into until they were face to face with whatever danger lurked.

"I'd like to stay here until I'm on my feet," Conner said, the certainty in his voice hadn't quite masked the immaturity of the situation. Sure, he was back and ready to join the service, but he was still young and clueless as to what he had to deal with here—not that any of that was Adam's business. That was all in the hands of their father and his brother.

Adam knew his place was the only other option he had, aside from their parents' place, but Adam also knew that it might do his brother good to stay there instead of in his place. That would most likely offer his father and brother little to no room to wade around their issue. They'd have to work it out one way or another before Conner got his own place.

Knowing that would make things worse, especially right away, Adam guided his brother upstairs to the spare bedroom, making sure they were quiet enough to not wake Ava, who definitely needed this nap because she was working on those terrible twos lately.

Laying the rules out for Conner as he checked them off on his fingers, he added, "No sneaking girls in and out of this house. We've got kids here and I'll be damned if you teach Tyler bad habits."

Conner gave a deep throated chuckle, followed up with a shitty grin like the sucker had actually thought about it prior to coming over. If there was anything Adam could try to manage was how his son treated women— more than a piece of fresh meat for the taking.

His brows furrowed as he gave a sharp stare at Conner. "I mean it."

"Okay, okay."

Conner held his hands up in defense as he backed himself away from Adam's death stare. "Tyler's of the age now where he's going to be picking up on bad habits, and I don't want him to learn them from you."

As though the statement had somehow offended him, Conner gave a raised look of innocence and said, "I wasn't planning on being my nephew's bad influence." He chucked his bags into the closet for the time being and said, "Hell, I'm nowhere near a bad influence."

They both got a good laugh out of those words before they made their way down the hallway toward the stairs. "I'm just saying... I don't want Tyler to get the idea that he can run away when things get hard."

If looks could kill, he'd be dead, but not until he reached the bottom of the stairs first. Turning back to face his brother on the landing, he met Conner—pissed off and ready to fight. Guarding himself with a busted up arm and one that wasn't his dominant, Adam called for a truce.

"Is that what you think I did?" his brother's voice was full of anger and stubbornness. "You think I just ran away and never looked back. You think it didn't frustrate me that this place couldn't offer me what I needed back then?"

Confusion mixed with an indescribable heat came over Adam as he stood a few feet from his brother before lashing out. "What did you expect us to believe when you left? It wasn't like you gave an explanation. If it was Dad, you could've stayed and worked it out instead of running off into the mountains of Colorado."

Pissed, Conner turned on his heel and made his way into the living room. "You think you have an idea, but you really have no clue, because yet again, everyone assumes what they don't fucking know."

Ava's voice broke through the madness in the living room. Adam turned to the stairs, and as he climbed, he looked at Conner. "This conversation isn't over."

It pained him to be having this heated argument with

his brother on his first day back home. And even though it wasn't truly his business as to why Conner had left in the first place, it was his family, and some would say that Adam was the peacemaker. He couldn't help wanting to solve whatever issue there had been, or was, between any of them. Their family was too good for fighting and not being close. It wasn't like the Jacobsen's to go this long with tension and fury separating them.

Chauffeuring Ava into the potty room, he assisted her with using her potty chair. Some had said that she might be too young, but she was grasping the concept quite well.

The last thing he wanted was for the kids to hear or see any of them arguing. He wasn't sure how much Ava had heard or even when she had woken up. She hadn't seemed too upset or concerned as they made their way to the stairs.

"Uncle Conner is here," he said, picking her up in order to carry her down the steep, carpeted stairs, which she wasn't too great at walking down quite yet.

"Unle Onner?"

"Yep, he's here to visit for a while," Adam said, unsure of his own words, because a part of him still wasn't sure if Conner would stay or leave, since the argument hadn't been too promising.

Rounding the banister, he set Ava on her feet and she went on a mission to find Uncle Conner. She didn't need to venture far, because he was standing on the back deck with his phone pressed against his ear, and an angry look on his face. He turned in the opposite direction, at the sight of Adam. Adam held out his hand to Ava. "He'll be in here soon. Let's get Ava some food."

The mention of food was enough to distract Ava as she

offered a slight fuss, but made her way into the kitchen. Her arms outstretched in front of the cereal cabinet. Knowing exactly what she wanted, Adam reached for the Cheerio container and poured her a bowlful. It hadn't taken him longer than a few days at home with her to know what Ava wanted and didn't want.

Following her into the living room, he set the bowl in front of her and turned on Sesame Street, a show she had to watch after naptime every day, no matter what. If he wasn't planning on going back to work soon, he would have programmed her favorite shows into the television according to her schedule.

The creak of the sliding door caught her attention, and before Adam could save the Cheerios, they spilled as she stood in order to race toward Uncle Conner with her arms outstretched, requesting to be picked up. Adam knelt down on the floor and did his best to gather the scattered cereal off the floor.

"Hey, I just got off the phone with Megan and she mentioned that I could talk with Liam about crashing above Levy's."

Standing from the floor, Adam carried the bowl to the garbage and emptied it. "Why? You've got a place here."

A pang of guilt struck Adam as he watched his brother's face twist with what looked like hurt and bent pride. Their argument hadn't been all that bad—it could have been a lot worse. Hell, they had grown up beating the hell out of one another, tossing in a few choice words when they had the opportunity between blows.

"I mean it."

Conner stood in front of him, holding Ava who was clinging tightly to the collar of his shirt—stretching it out with just the grip of her fist. "I don't know. I'll have to think about it."

"Come on, there's nothing to think about," Adam offered a fresh bowl of Cheerios to Ava, who now insisted Conner put her down. He placed her in front of the television, where Ernie was singing to his rubber duck. Adam placed the bowl in front of her and turned back to Conner, who was now leaning against the frame of the sliding doors. "I'm not looking to fight about anything."

A quizzical look crossed Conner's face, and Adam knew he was recalling what had happened prior to Ava waking up. "Well, aside from that."

A shrug was always Conner's first response to anything he wasn't sure about. Adam knew him like the back of his hand. They had the same attitude when it came down to it. Probably the reason they had fought all the time. "I'll think about it."

Ignoring his brother's words, Adam said, "When are you thinking about starting on the squad?"

Pushing off the wall, Conner grabbed a chair at the table and slid it out. "As soon as I can, but I know there's orientation and what not, so..."

"You know the place inside and out. You won't need the extensive training the other newbies get."

"Okay, then," Conner said, clasping his hands together. "Looks like I'll be good to go whenever you give the word."

"I'll make some calls and set it up," Adam said, pulling his phone out of his pocket. He knew the guys would be happy to hear they had more help coming, along with someone who would be knowledgeable and worth a damn—at least, Adam hoped his brother would live up to those expectations and not run when things didn't go his way.

Conner turned in his chair and faced him with a look of unease before saying, "I wish I had been here sooner, ya know?"

Adam knew what he was referring to. The day of the explosion, Conner had mentioned to Rachel that he felt he owed something to Adam for not being there.

"It should've been me pulling you away from death, not some *girl*," Conner said, oblivious that he was laughing at his own joke, which Adam found no humor in.

"Megan's damned good at what she does," Adam said, admitting that she was probably the best one they had on the team, when it came to doing what needed done and not thinking twice.

Conner swallowed hard, choking on words as he stammered his way through an explanation of what he had meant to say. Adam held a hand up, not caring to hear exactly how his brother had meant to make a strike against the one who had saved his life. Regardless of how many people were on standby for medical, it had been Megan who had switched gears and kicked ass to do what she did best. He wasn't going to allow anyone, including his brother, say anything different, regardless of guilt or hurt pride or whatever his brother was feeling for not being there.

24

*O*ffering vanilla cupcakes with pink filled frosting and extravagant sprinkles on top, Rachel carried in two boxes and placed them on the pink clothed fold out tables near the back of the room.

Rachel smiled at the sight of Leah waddling over to her. The woman was ready to pop, like an overinflated balloon waiting for the right moment to surprise everyone.

"They look amazing, Rach," Leah said, standing next to the table as she pried open a lid in order to grab one out. "I've been dying to try one since mentioning them. Granny Mae is lucky I didn't break into the café last night to rob the freezer."

Laughing along with her, Rachel offered her a napkin from nearby and said, "I think we're all lucky that didn't happen."

Leah held the cupcake out to the side as she hugged Rachel. They had put off the baby shower until today. A

Saturday that promised nothing but pink ribbons and gift bags to welcome the new little Spencer girl—whose name would be Willow Mae, and who would be surrounded by love from all around.

"I have to run out and grab my gift," Rachel said, making sure that Leah wouldn't open any gifts until she was back. Ava reached for the container of cupcakes, wanting another one even though she'd had more than enough already. Leah shooed Rachel off in the direction of the door before giving Ava exactly what she wanted.

Rachel had no choice but to chuckle as she made her way out to the parking lot. Of course, Auntie Lee would give her little girl everything and anything she wanted. Ava had her wrapped around those little fingers of hers.

She had Leah's gift wrapped and tucked inside a bag, just to be sure there'd be no peaking beforehand. Having a little girl of her own, she knew how important keepsakes were and keeping track of their firsts. She carried the bag into the room and set it down next to Leah, who was coercing Ava to hand her gifts in exchange for a bite of a cupcake. Leave it to Leah to bribe a child with more sweets than the child's tummy could possibly handle.

Rachel stood close by, camera in hand as Leah unwrapped her gift. It was a necessity to catch the rush of emotion that was about to happen as Leah undid the last of the wrapping paper and saw what the gift was. Leah's eyes beamed as a smile spread across her face, followed with brimming tears as she pulled out the diaper bag filled with everything she could possibly need, including a tiny scrapbook for the baby's firsts.

"Rach," she managed to say, despite her trembling lips and inability to say anything more.

Rachel snapped a picture, receiving a look from Leah promising payback. Wanting to hug her best friend, she first had to help her stand before wrapping her arms around her and pulling her close. "I'm so happy for you, and I can't wait to meet Willow Mae."

AFTER SPENDING the last hour helping Leah haul everything home from the baby shower, Rachel and Ava pulled into the driveway. It was nice to finally be home. She was more than ready to relax.

The guys were in the backyard with Tyler, playing football. Adam was doing his best with the one arm he had to work with. Rachel pulled open the sliding door and slid out onto the back deck.

Conner tossed the ball back to Tyler, who was now dodging and weaving between his uncle and father, trying to make an imaginary touchdown on the other end of the lawn.

Ava stood on the edge of the steps alongside the baby gate, clapping at the touchdown her big brother had just made. Adam turned his attention on her, and before he had a chance to reach her, she was running toward Rachel's chair in order to get away from him. Adam climbed over the gate and pretended he couldn't find Ava. "Where'd she go? I can't see her?"

Ava sat quietly in Rachel's lap as she dug her face into her mother's shirt—her fair attempt at hiding from Adam. It hadn't lasted long once Adam announced the tickle monster would be able to find her. Ava bounced off

Rachel's lap and ran the opposite direction of Adam's outstretched hands.

The tiny screams echoed; ricocheting off the side of the house as Adam cornered her, allowing her no way to escape being tickled. She watched on with amusement as Ava kicked and squirmed her way free of Adam's torturing tickles. She couldn't go too far before he grabbed her once again with one arm and twirled her around in a circle, causing her to shriek in delight and laughter.

Conner reached out once Adam stopped and tickled Ava's belly, which was now sticking out from under her shirt. "I'm going to get you," Conner said, pouncing in the direction Ava ran. The look on her face told Rachel she wasn't having it. A short fuss and scream later, Conner called it quits. "Okay, I'll stop." He offered a hand out and asked, "Can we still be friends?"

Ava stuck a thumb in her mouth and rubbed her free hand against her tired eyes. "Someone sleepy?" Rachel asked, not expecting Ava to admit to being tired. Usually she put up a fight and refused taking a nap. This time, Rachel walked her up the stairs and placed her in the center of her big girl bed, tucking her in with her favorite quilt that grandma had made for her.

Walking back outside, she told Adam that she needed to run to the café to make sure the cupcakes were ready for tomorrow's big day. He offered to keep an eye on the kids while she ran in to town, as she promised it wouldn't take longer than a few minutes once she was there.

When he kissed her, he purposely let his lips trail to familiar territory, causing her to squirm right there on the back porch. Trying to hide what he did to her, she turned away from him and pulled open the door before attempting to escape the hold he had on her. He followed her inside, closed the door, and pressed her up against the wall.

"Stop," she pleaded, pointing in the direction of the back door. "They're out there."

He shrugged against her, pressing his lips hard against her neck, allowing his teeth to graze against the skin as he pulled her into the kitchen, out of view of Tyler and Conner. "And we're in here." His words and breath hot against her neck.

Her head fell back against the cabinet as he lifted her onto the counter, pressing his hardened length, suppressed by denim, against her. She couldn't deny how badly she wanted what he had to offer. Between the pills and the injuries that had kept him from any activity, it had been a while since they had been intimate, and the tension between them had been evident, even more so now, as he ravished her with his hands and mouth.

With one strong swipe, he had her over his shoulder and was carrying her toward the stairs. Digging her fingers into his back on the way up the stairs, she heard his grunt as he placed her on their bed. He undressed her with his eyes first as he tossed his own clothes aside, leaving a pile on the floor.

Taking her own initiative to undress herself, she pulled at the button of her shorts and slid them down her thighs, allowing him to strip her free of what blocked him from seeing her lying naked in front of him.

A low growl was heard as he pulled her hips closer to

him and entered her in one fluid motion, promising her much more than a quick escape as he thrummed his thumb along the spot of no return. Arching into him, she allowed him to take her to that point and back—over and over again, until they were both sent over the edge and left in the afterglow of sweat and bliss.

25

*B*eing injured and on the mend had set him back a few weeks. Now, with the town's baking festival set up and ready to go, his plan was shoved back until another time—which was okay, because no one wanted to see a man with only one usable arm propose to a beautiful woman like Rachel. No matter what her answer would be, it'd still look pitiful on his part.

Liam had called it like he saw it as Adam walked into Levy's. "Haven't figured it out yet?"

The place had picked up since nine that morning and Liam had told him to stop in to talk through some things. Adam knew what things, or perhaps thing, Liam was referring to.

He pulled a barstool away from the bar and took a seat. There wasn't time for drinking, with the parade about to start in less than thirty minutes or so. He had left his brother in charge of lining up the trucks while he took a quick break to clear his head.

Tyler had stayed back with Conner, and Rachel had Ava helping prepare the stand with her up and coming prize winning cupcakes. They all knew she'd win with those buttercream frosted chocolate treats.

The town was buzzing with excitement over this festival and here he sat, wishing he'd get some courage to get his crap together.

"Here's what I think you need to do," Liam said, offering Adam a glass of Pepsi on ice. Adam took a drink, hoping there would be something stronger mixed with it, but he hadn't been that lucky. He wouldn't complain though, the ice cold drink cooled him down from the heat of the mid-summer sun he'd been in all morning. "I still think you should propose when you have the chance."

Adam didn't like the idea of winging it. Something would go wrong and then the whole surprise of the proposal would be blown. Not that planning things always went the way they were planned, but still... it was a chance he was willing to take.

"I'm thinkin' you should do it when she's least expecting it. Kind of like what I did with Leah," Liam said, with a smirk plastered on his face.

"I'm thinkin' I should just keep thinkin'," Adam said, taking a long drink before saying, "I'm just not sure when the right time is."

Liam shrugged, and even though Adam knew he had something more to say, he watched Liam walk down to the other end of the bar and say something to Adam's grandfather, who in turn, looked down at Adam and asked, "What are ya waitin' for, boy? Go put a ring on that woman before someone beats ya to it."

Liam glanced down at him, smirk still plastered on his face, and offered Adam a reassuring "That's what I think, too" look.

He decided he would take their advice. No sense in waiting around for the right moment when the right moment may never come. Better now than never.

Climbing off the barstool, he tipped back what was left of the Pepsi and waved in their direction as he headed for the door. If a proposal was what everyone wanted, it would be a proposal they would get... as soon as he figured out when and where.

Rachel had never been so nervous in her life. She wasn't a pro, yet the ladies swore she was. They had included her in their registration at the bake off, telling everyone, including the judges, that they had no idea what they were in for. Doris had offered a sample to one of the judges prior to the festival kick off, but it had been hush hush because they all knew how illegal that had been.

They had placed their table front and center, lined with cupcakes and a few other frosted treats. Their prize winner would be the buttercream frosted cupcakes with a glaze of sprinkled sugar and walnuts on top—or so the ladies had said that morning, when they had been helping Rachel with the table.

The emcee announced over the loudspeaker that it was time for the judges to receive their desserts. At this time, she shooed Ava off in the direction of Tyler, who was sitting front and center of the stage. He reached for

Ava and set her in his lap as they both gave Rachel a thumbs up.

Rachel's nerves thrashed and her stomach flip-flopped about as she watched the judges take a bite of each cupcake, taking time with each one, being sure to take another bite if there was any doubt on where the cupcake stood as far as taste. They conversed amongst themselves, keeping their voices soft as whispers. One had even gone so far as whispering behind her notecard.

This was intense. Nothing like Rachel had thought it would be. Sure, she had known there would be judges and what not, but nothing like this. She thought it would have been something fun and quick, not serious with deliberate judging.

The judges were as serious as those in a courtroom, deliberating and discussing the taste and every minute detail of each cupcake—as though it would be life or death.

The ladies of her "cupcake tribe" from Granny Mae's fidgeted and squabbled beside her. Francine almost shouted for the judges to hurry up and make a decision already, and she would have, if Granny Mae hadn't kept her seated with a hand over her mouth.

The judges still had three more entries to try, which meant Rachel's, along with everyone else's, nerves would be fried by the time the verdict was in.

ADAM HAD NEVER BEEN as nervous as he was now. The parade had ended and now he was standing among the crowd gathered around the bake off contest.

He spotted Rachel right away in the crowd of contestants. The way she ran her teeth over her bottom lip told him how nervous she was—something he had picked up on when they had first started dating.

As if she could feel his eyes on her, she turned in his direction and gave him a quick nervous wave. There was no doubt in his mind that he wanted to make that beautiful blonde woman his for the rest of his life.

Giving her a wink in return that he knew would cause her a whole new set of butterflies, he made his way to Tyler and Ava, taking a seat next to a few husbands who were more than eager to get on with their day.

Where most husbands sat bored, he sat in admiration of the one he loved as he contemplated his next move.

It had taken the judges more than an hour to announce the winner. He swore he had seen actual court proceed faster than that. What the hell was so hard in choosing the best cupcake?

The judges sat in their assigned seats before deciding on which one of them would make the announcement. Finally, one of them, a dark haired woman with freckles and glasses asked the contestants to approach their tables.

He could see the sweat glistening on Rachel's face, reminding him of the intimate moments they had recently shared. Taking his thoughts away from that, he thought about how badly Rachel wanted the win for the ladies at the café.

"Ladies and Gentlemen," the freckle faced woman announced before clearing her throat. "There was a good selection of contestants today and a lot of great-tasting cupcakes, too. Which made it a bit of a challenge to choose just one winner."

This was straight torture. The amount of time they had taken, he could have proposed three times over again.

"I just want to take an extra minute and thank everyone for participating in the bake off this year," the woman said, obviously wanting to draw this event out and keep everyone on the edge of their seats. "Without further ado, I will announce the winner. The winner will receive a check in the amount of ten thousand dollars."

Stalling long enough to drive the crowd to restlessness and demanding shouts, the woman finally announced, "The winner is Rachel Elliot and her team from Granny Mae's Café."

The woman fumbled the mic as she tried to clap along with the crowd. She moved to the side as the festival's director, who happened to be the town mayor, presented Rachel and the others with a check. They held their pose for a few minutes longer, making sure pictures captured the moment for the local newspaper and the town's website.

Rachel's smile was knockout gorgeous as she stood on the stage, accepting the win with a polite "thank you" to each of the judges. What she said next surprised him. It wasn't supposed to be her surprising him...

"On behalf of Granny Mae's and the rest of the community," she said, fixing her eyes on him as she said every word. "With this check, and the multitude of donations received, we would like to present the money to the CVFD."

The festival's director turned their attention to the crowd, following Rachel's pointed finger in Adam's direction, and called him up to the stage.

26

*A*nnouncing the donations go to the Cedar Valley Fire Department had made everything worth it. The look on Adam's face as he made his way up to the stage, she knew it had made his day.

Tyler sat with Ava in the crowd, both of them clapping and Ava babbling incessantly without a clue as to what had truly happened and why her mother was on stage with tears in her eyes.

Regardless of winning or not, this moment would have happened, and that thought alone made Rachel proud to be a part of this community. They had pulled together to make this happen and it had, without any trouble at all.

What she hadn't expected to happen, happened right after Adam thanked the town of Cedar Valley, along with his gorgeous girlfriend, on behalf of him and the fire department.

"Ever since the day I had met Rachel, I knew that she was something special," he said, offering her that sly wink of his, which would always set her heart racing. "The baking was just an added bonus, along with Ava, her beautiful, curly blonde haired little girl, who has stolen my heart right along with her mother. I couldn't have asked for anyone better to come into Tyler's and my life."

Turning to Rachel, he reached for her hand and held tight as he continued with his swoon-worthy speech. "Rachel has been nothing but the best for Tyler. Offering her patience and warm guidance, teaching him and nurturing him as a mother would," he said, and at that very moment, Rachel could see the tears that had gathered in his eyes. "There is no doubt in my mind that I want to spend the rest of my life with her."

Adam turned to face her for what she had thought was just a kiss, but instead, he dropped to one knee while fishing something out of his pocket.

Standing speechless in front of him as he pulled a small black box out and opened it, Rachel couldn't wait to answer with a yes. She had been waiting for this moment since the first time she had met him.

"Rachel, I want you to be the one I wake up to every morning and the one I kiss goodnight. I want you to be mine for as long as I live. Will you marry me?"

"Yes, Adam Jacobsen, I will marry you." Pulling him up by a tug of her hand, she wrapped her arms around him and whispered in his ear, "You didn't think I could have possibly ever said no, did you?"

"You're engaged?!" Leah shouted into the phone. It was a good thing Rachel didn't need her hearing much anymore. "I can't believe he finally asked you! He and Liam have been talking about it forever! And of course, I missed it because of the heat!"

Holding the phone away from her ear to save some of her hearing, Rachel said, "Yes, he finally asked. And of course I said yes, because there isn't anyone else I'd rather be with."

She didn't care how cliché or cheesy it sounded, because it was true. There had been a few men she thought were "the one," but they had instantly proved her wrong, before she had even gotten her hopes up, Scott included.

"We're going to celebrate once I have this baby," Leah promised, her voice much calmer than it had been. "Which will be soon enough if these contractions get closer together."

The thought of Leah having contractions should have trumped anything else Rachel had to offer in the conversation, but it wouldn't. "I'm afraid that won't happen so soon."

"What? The contractions getting closer and more agonizing?"

Rachel hesitated, giving a minute for what she had said to Leah to sink in. She didn't have to wait too long before Leah's shrieks were heard even as she pulled the phone away.

"Rach, are you serious?" Leah's voice an octave higher than she had first started out with. "When did this happen?"

"Well, there was this time when..." She had yet to tell Adam, who would find out later that night when she would surprise him with a bag containing a t-shirt, a onesie and the positive pregnancy test.

"I mean, how far along are you, smartass," Leah said, sounding like she was hyperventilating.

"Take a breath, Lee," Rachel said, realizing something wasn't right.

"I'm trying, but something just happened..."

"What? What just happened?" Rachel clung desperately to the phone in her hand as she pressed it hard against her ear, willing Leah to say something—anything. "Lee, what happened?"

"My water just broke."

THIS DAY WAS sure to go down in history, double marks on the calendar worth keeping for both sides of the family. Rachel's engagement was now shared with the birth of Willow Mae Spencer, a bright eyed and beautiful chestnut-brown haired baby with eyes the color of the sky mixed with a crescent of golden brown that matched her mother's.

Another baby to love and spoil, finally making her an auntie she never would have been if it hadn't been for Leah. "She's perfect," Rachel said, when she finally got the chance to meet her.

Leah patted a spot beside her and motioned for Rachel to have a seat. Rachel obliged as she sat on the edge and scooted up closer to Leah. She couldn't help but get emotional as she looked down over the bundle in her arms. Liam and Leah had a perfect daughter and she couldn't wait for girl days full of shopping and getting their hair and nails done.

"I need to talk to Rosie about planning your wedding," Leah mentioned, while she fed her little girl. "Have you guys set a date yet?"

She hadn't even thought of a date. He'd just proposed for Pete's sake. They wouldn't be married for at least another year or so, unless of course Adam married her sooner because of the baby on the way...

"Like, next month, or maybe in the fall?" Leah asked, persistent on figuring out the details right this minute, ignoring the fact that she'd just had a baby, and should be sleeping or something.

"Lee, relax," Rachel said, nudging her arm into Leah's. "We'll set a date when we actually have a chance to talk about it. Right now, all you need to focus on is Willow. She's all that matters right now."

Leah's eyes filled with tears as she looked at Rachel, who was now making her way to a chair at the end of the bed. Nurses needed to take the baby and get footprints and other newborn baby things they do when the baby is less than a day old. "You're going to have a baby," Leah whispered, as tears silently slipped free.

Apparently, the drugs that were given to Leah during the labor of Willow were still in her system, because Rachel didn't remember acting this way after the birth of Ava. Unless, of course, the drugs kept her from remembering it. Rachel looked around for any sign of Liam or Adam being in close proximity of the room. The last thing she wanted was for Adam to find out through overhearing Leah's one-sided conversation. Holding a finger to her lips, Rachel whispered, "Shh... It's supposed to be a surprise."

Leah's lips trembled, tears fell uncontrollably, and

Rachel knew that she needed to leave her be. She needed a nap—she was exhausted and overwhelmed from the labor and delivery of her little girl. The sleep would help Leah become normal again, once the drugs were out of her system. Right now, they were strong and not mixing well with Leah's hormones.

The guys walked into the room shortly after Rachel stood to give Leah a hug goodbye. She turned to Liam and mouthed "I'll be back later or tomorrow. She needs some rest." He nodded okay with his thumb up and held the door open while giving Adam a pat on his back on the way out.

Rachel would have liked to stay there longer, but remembering how busy the first few hours were after the birth, along with the emotions running high, and not to forget the exhaustion and fatigue of the whole thing, she knew Leah needed it quiet and Liam would take care of her. She was in good hands.

Adam held the door open for Rachel as she climbed into the passenger seat of his truck. They had the night to themselves. The kids were with Adam's parents for the night, allowing Adam and Rachel time to do whatever they wanted. Several thoughts of what to do crossed Rachel's mind, but there was only one that took precedence over the remaining things that could wait for a while. She couldn't wait to get home.

PULLING INTO THE DRIVEWAY, her heart raced and butterflies came alive as they flittered and bounced their way around her stomach. The amount of excitement and nervousness caused her stomach to feel sick as it flipped.

"Hey, what's the matter?"

Swallowing down the feeling of getting sick, Rachel offered a smile and explanation. "Nothing, just thinking of everything that happened today. It all just hit me, that's all."

He took hold of her hand and pulled her close to him along the bench seat of his truck. Scooting along the seat without objection, Rachel snuggled into Adam's chest; her thoughts of what his expression would be at the news of expecting. Where she had once been nervous, she was now feeling a leap of excitement, and couldn't wait to find out. She wanted so much for them. With everything that had happened today, she might as well toss in the surprise for him—as though he hadn't been surprised enough, and vice versa, but this surprise would trump all the others tenfold and there would be no doubt that this day would forever be engrained in their memories.

They had plenty of time to pick dates and celebrate their engagement. She didn't want to rush through it. They'd have plenty of time to get the details figured out. Right now, she needed to get him inside to show him what she had been anxiously waiting to show him for the last few days.

"Rach," he said, her name sounded forced, like he was trying to find his words without hesitating too long. She looked up at him. His eyelids were heavy, with dark bags underneath; evidence of his lack of sleep and the worry that had played its way into their lives within the last month. "I really wish I could have had one of your cupcakes today."

She released a sigh of relief. That wasn't what she thought he was going to say. A part of her had thought maybe he was recanting his proposal. That he was having second thoughts. She had thought doubts had found their way into his thoughts soon after he realized what he had done. She could handle the whole cupcake situation.

He followed her into the house after grabbing the mail, giving her plenty of time to grab the surprise bag out of the closet. It was a surprise in itself that he or the kids hadn't gotten into the closet and found it. She was glad they hadn't. This was the perfect time to let him know they were expecting, yet another thing to look forward to in the near future.

She carried the bag into the living room, where he was sitting in his favorite recliner, opening the mail and tossing the unimportant stuff to the side. She held up the bag, which was a neutral color with a large question mark on the front. Of course, she knew it was a bag that couples used for gender reveal parties, where everyone gathered around to find out the sex of the baby while the parents had known all along. The thought to do that had crossed her mind, but she knew she wouldn't be able to keep it secret for too long. The other thought she had had was for the ultrasound tech to be the only one to know that day and seal it in an envelope. But Rachel knew the envelope wouldn't last long.

"What's that?" He was sitting forward with his elbows on his knees now, eyes on the bag she had carried into the living room. "Is that for Leah and her baby?"

Shaking her head, she placed it in front of him, and sat at his feet. The nerves that weren't fried from earlier were now buzzing and causing her to feel queasy once again. "It's for you."

His eyebrows drew together as he pulled apart the seal of the bag and reached in. "What's this for?"

Offering a subtle shrug, she waited for him to pull the items out. Confusion crossed his face as he pulled out the folded t-shirt and the pack of cigars. More than likely the cigars threw him off because he wasn't a smoker, but she couldn't leave them out. The pack of cigars is what wrapped up the package with the conclusion of a need to celebrate.

He unfolded the t-shirt, finding the folded onesie inside. He unfolded both and held them up to read them. He dropped them in his lap and looked at her. A smile broke his confused expression. "We're expecting?"

She nodded slowly, with an identical smile on her face. She was lifted off the floor in one swift motion and into his lap. "We're going to have a baby?"

As though sitting was no longer an option through the excitement, Adam stood, spinning her around and kissing her—passionately and full of desire.

"How far along are you?" he asked, setting her back down on her own two feet.

She didn't know how far along she was, because she had only taken the pregnancy test after a bout of sickness hit her a while ago, between checking on Adam at the hospital and baking cupcakes and other sweet treats for the diner. She knew that something was going on when licking the spoon after whipping up frosting had caused her to get sick.

"I'm not sure. I wouldn't think I'm too far along."

He wrapped his arm around her and pulled her close.

His lips met her forehead where they stayed for longer than a minute. Thoughts overwhelmed her of what the two of them, all of them, were going to experience—together as one.

He placed his hand on her stomach, where nothing more than a small bump had formed in the last week, another indication that made her think the scale was broken or that she was gaining weight from eating too many sweets. "Maybe it's twins in there."

"Don't press your luck," she said, pointing a warning finger at him. Not that the thought of twins was a bad thing. She had always wanted to experience having twins, something she had played around with since she was younger with twin dolls. She had begged her parents to buy her two of everything just so she could have twin babies. Now, the thought of having two of everything caused her to grimace in expected aches and pains of carrying two babies.

"I think it'd be great," Adam said, rubbing her stomach, mumbling something to it as if his words would miraculously place two babies inside.

"Would you like to carry them?"

He looked down at her stomach and once again mumbled something, recanting his wish for more than one baby. She laughed. "You're too much. What am I going to do with you?"

"The same thing you've been doing with me," he said, trailing his lips along her neck, finding the soft spot between her neck and shoulder. Her head tipped back, hormones doubling the effect of the scent of his cologne and the way he made her feel.

he visit to the doctor ended with the removal of his cast. After x-rays and a follow up exam, the doctor had okayed the removal of the cast and his return to work. The only restriction the doctor had noted was for Adam to take it easy. No heavy lifting. He wanted Adam to give his arm a chance to fully recover. The muscles were still weak and would be for a bit longer.

Adam promised Rachel that morning that he would mind the doctor's orders. He didn't want to end up back in a cast. He couldn't wait any longer to get back to the station. Visits here and there during his time off had done little to calm his worries about upholding the department.

He hadn't seen Conner in the last few days. The guy had been staying at the station, pulling doubles and making sure everything was taken care of. His brother had come a long way since the last time they'd had a chance to talk. If Adam hadn't thought about it before, he was definitely thinking it now.

Conner greeted him at the door. He was antsy and

eager to show him around. He wanted to show him what he had done to the place, swearing that the changes were nothing too drastic and they were a good thing.

Adam followed him through the station, glancing over things, but not paying too close attention to it. He wasn't at all worried about the changes Conner had made. It was probably for the better and he shouldn't have doubted Conner so much in the past.

"The place looks great," Adam said, noticing the extra space in the sleeping room and the new set of lockers instead of hooks for everyone's stuff. "You've done good for the place."

Conner wasn't the young boy Adam remembered. He stood six feet and broad shouldered. His face had transformed from the boyish grin to one more masculine. His voice was deeper and there was no denying the fact that he was ready to get his shit together.

"I figured it was time to earn my keep around here," he said, jabbing an elbow at Adam. "You guys have been great to me since I came back and since I'm new around here, I wanted to stay low key for a while. Didn't want to make sudden moves and wind up getting my ass handed to me."

Adam had a laugh at that. The kid had nothing to worry about when it came to that. There wasn't anyone here at the department who would beat him up for making changes. Everyone he talked to was more than glad Conner was here to pick up some of the extra hours and the slack caused by injuries and things out of their control.

"It's great to have you here," Adam said, offering a pat on his brother's back before walking toward the office. "As long as you keep your head on straight and focused on what you really want, there won't be any problems around here."

He wasn't referring to those problems between their father and Conner. Those problems would eventually work themselves out. Given some time, a rather large amount of alcohol, and less amount of stubbornness, they'd most likely forget what they were so angered about in the first place. It wasn't like the Jacobsen's to hold grudges. Anger wasn't worth the destruction of holding onto it.

"You know I talked to Dad the other day?"

No, Adam hadn't heard. With everything happening this week, along with the news of a little one on the way, he hadn't paid much attention to anything besides his own little family. Tyler had gone off to camp with his buddies and Ava was still working through the terrible twos. She was getting more and more ornery with each passing day, giving him a run for his title as father as he learned how to deal with little girls and their tantrums.

"He said he'd like to have a longer talk," Conner said, ignoring the fact that Adam had spaced out of their conversation. "I'm not so sure what to say to him."

Adam wasn't sure what to say to his father either. It used to be simple to strike up a conversation with the man, but lately, his moods were too much and you never knew what kind of mood he was in. It was like walking on egg shells, which he didn't mind once in a while, but it made him feel for his mother, who had no choice but put up with it day in and day out.

"It's hard to say. I suggest just being upfront and honest with him, like he has been with us," Adam said, grabbing the stack of mail on the desk. Glancing up, he caught Conner in mid-thought, "I know it won't be easy, but you have to try. That's about all you can do."

His father refused to go to the doctor. Their fear that there was an underlying condition causing him to have these unnecessary mood swings and outbursts were no concern to his father. He said there was nothing wrong— he'd like to enjoy his retirement without so much as a peep about problems. He told them he had enough to worry about. Well, whatever it was he was worried about, he sure wasn't going to tell any of them, including Adam's mother.

"I just have a bad feeling," Conner said, pulling up a chair next to the desk, motioning for Adam to do the same. "I've had this feeling for a while now. It bugged me every now and then when I'd call home to talk to Mom. She'd pretend everything was okay, but the night I came back for dinner, I could tell things had changed."

The thought of Conner coming back because of trouble at home and not because he truly wanted to be here worried Adam. What if tomorrow or the next day Conner decided to up and leave again? Not that Adam had any say in what his brother did, he just thought it was nice having him back home.

"Is that what made you come back home?" Adam asked, trying to keep his own insecurities out of the conversation.

Conner wrapped his hand around the paperweight on the desk and balanced it in his hand while he figured out what to say next. Adam could always tell when his brother had a lot on his mind, because he had to have something in his hands the time it took him to talk it all out.

"Sure, that was one of the reasons I decided to come

back," Conner offered just enough to keep Adam guessing what was coming next.

"What are the other reasons?"

With a subtle shrug, followed by the plop of the paperweight, Conner stood, sliding his chair back as he made his way out of the office. Adam had no choice but to put the mail he had been holding down and follow his brother. "Wait, where are ya goin'?" he called out, rounding the corner of the kitchen, following after Conner like a stray dog.

Taking a detour to the back of the station, he watched his brother as he entered the sleeping area, opened a locker and pulled out a stack of papers that looked as disheveled as his expression. He handed them to Adam, who in turn sifted through them, scanning them with confusion. Trying to make sense as to why his brother was showing him articles and pictures, his brows tugged together as he looked up at Conner. "What's all this?"

"Articles from the paper."

Obviously, that's what they were. Adam could tell that. What he couldn't understand is what they were for or why his brother had them. "I can see that."

Pulling the stack from Adam's hands, Conner flipped through the crumpled sheets of paper until he found one he was looking for. Pulling it free away from the others, he held it out for Adam to grab hold of. Adam read the headline.

Now it made sense. There had been a big forest fire that had taken the lives of several firemen out in Colorado. It had taken a heavy toll on the count at the station out there. Adam had seen it on the news. He had called Conner to make sure he had been all right, not thinking about the after effects of this fire and how they would affect his brother.

"Remember when I packed up the day before I left home?"

How could he forget? He hadn't been an emotional man, but the thought of the distance that would separate him from his brother had been a bit overwhelming. He hated the fact that they'd be so far away from each other, making it seem almost impossible to stay in touch or close for that matter. They had managed for the last few years, but it had definitely taken a toll on their relationships.

"Yeah, I remember," Adam said, taking another look at the article in his hands. The fatalities had climbed to nearly thirty. It had been the largest fire the state of Colorado had ever seen. The panic he and his parents had felt while watching the news that night, knowing that Conner was battling those flames right along with those losing their lives.

"Do you remember what I said?" Conner questioned him, taking a seat on the edge of the bed. Arms resting on his knees as he leaned forward, waiting for Adam to recall the memory of the night before Conner had taken off. The night he had proclaimed that there was more in life waiting for him to discover. If he stayed in Cedar Valley, he would miss the chance of a lifetime.

"Yeah, I remember."

They had let him leave, without any more fight to give, they had all watched Conner load his truck up and head out on the highway, unsure if they'd ever hear from him again.

"Well, I'm taking that all back."

Adam looked at him like he had lost his mind. "You can't take back what you said that long ago. Words are the last thing you can ever take back. The damage is already done."

Those were fighting words. Adam knew that and so did Conner. The look on Conner's face said it all. He didn't have to say a damned thing for Adam to know what he was thinking.

"Look, I ain't looking for a fight," Conner said, holding his hands up. "I didn't come back to fight with you guys. I came back to make up for lost time."

The irk was there, causing heat to spread under Adam's skin. There would never be a better time than now to get this all out in the open, whether it would cause another issue or not, they'd soon find out.

"I thought Colorado was the place to be," Conner explained, not giving Adam a chance to interrupt. "At first it was great, I won't lie about that. Chasing huge fires and car accidents involving falling boulders..."

His words trailed off and Adam could see he was thinking back on the good calls, the ones that went well and ended successfully. "Then the fires were getting larger, getting harder to control," he said, pointing toward the article in Adam's hand. "That fire took a lot of manpower to try to control it, but it ended up taking a helluva lot more than that once it was done spreading its ugly flames across the land."

Realizing how beat up his brother had gotten over this fire that had made national news, made him realize he might have been a bit too harsh and uptight with him. His brother deserved some slack for having to face what he did out in Colorado.

"I lost friends that were family, and family that wasn't friendly that year," he said, again pointing at the article in Adam's hands. "Hearing about the fire out at Woodland's farm and the explosion that tossed you aside..."

His brother choked on the emotion as it unleashed and forced its escape. There was nothing left to do except hug him and pull in close. His little brother had been beat up and spit out by the ugliness of the reality firefighters had to face from time to time.

"I thought I lost you, man," Conner said, his face beet red, anger twisting his mouth as emotions pressed on.

"But you didn't. I'm right here." Adam wrapped his strong arm around his brother and pulled him into his side. Guilt edged its ugly sword into Adam's gut as he thought about the hell his brother had gone through. The hell they had both gone through, at the news of each other's battle of fires. They had both been afraid of losing the other, but hadn't spoken a word to one another, until they realized how close death had come to destroying their chance to make things right.

Whoever said grown men don't cry was full of shit. There had been enough tears shed to last them a while. But it had felt good to get it all out, making their relationship that much stronger. If he had known his brother wasn't happy out in Colorado, he would have tried a heck of a lot harder to get him back home.

"I hope you're not planning on going anywhere for a while," he offered, as they walked out of the room and headed for the bay.

"Why's that?"

Adam shot him a glance that, if he had to guess, told his brother not to mess around.

Conner held his hands up in defense. "I'm not going anywhere, Jesus, settle down."

"Because you're going to be meeting a niece or nephew soon."

A brow rose and the sarcasm followed. "How soon we talkin'? Will I have time to make a trip back..."

A slug in his arm shut him up. "Ow, what was that for?"

"You aren't leaving, ever. You're home for good. We need you here."

Having his brother around would ease the stress and the worry. He would allow Conner to implement some of the training he'd had out in Colorado. It was a good thing Conner was back home, no matter what their father had to say about it.

A few months later...

The envelope received was from Adam's friend, Lux Hamilton, who had promised Adam he'd do some checking around as far as the custody battle over Ava was concerned.

She had forgotten about the whole situation, or at least had put it on the back burner, since she hadn't heard anything from Scott's attorney in the last couple of months.

Opening the envelope and reading through the paper Lux had sent, it was clear why she hadn't heard anything since she received the very first paper. The attorneys had been working behind the scenes in an attempt to come to an agreement on an immediate mediation for Scott, Rachel and Ava.

She didn't want to keep Ava from Scott. It had been his own actions that had kept him away from her. Seeking a lawyer to handle this was irrational and a bit uncalled for on Scott's behalf. This was something that could have been handled without the court's help.

"What's that?" Adam asked, walking in from outside. Since his arm was more than healed, basically back to normal, he had been catching up on missed yard time with Tyler.

"Lux sent me this," she said, handing the paper over so he could check it out. "This could've been handled without lawyers."

"I agree, but it's one of the benefits of having an attorney as a good friend," Adam said, holding the paper up as proof. "He basically worked it out for us and all I have to do is return the favor."

Rachel slid, defeated, into the kitchen chair. "I know, it's not exactly what you wanted, but it could've been a lot worse," he said, wrapping an arm around her.

She knew he was right. Scott had dealt this hand and it ended up being a win-win for all involved. It was just the fact that he didn't know Ava.

"I know, it's just that it's not right for him to waltz into her life whenever it's convenient for him," she explained, trying her damnedest to make Adam understand. "Missing out on two years of her life is a big deal. He's basically a stranger to Ava."

Adam pulled a chair away from the table and sat down next to her. "You're right. I couldn't imagine missing two years of my child's life, but I give him credit for wanting to be in it now."

Rachel pushed back, crossing her arms in front of her chest. "Whose side are you on?"

"Rach," he said, grabbing hold of her hand, breaking apart her arms from their position. "There are no sides in this. It's what's best for Ava. That's the only thing that matters to me."

Nodding because she had to agree, she leaned forward and reached for the paper. Picking up the phone, she dialed the number provided on the sheet and waited for Lux to answer.

IT WAS A DONE DEAL. Sign on the line and follow the rules. She could do that, right? She couldn't guarantee there would be a lack of tears or an emotional outburst the first weekend Scott picked Ava up from their house, but she knew she would manage to get through it. She didn't have any other choice.

Leaving Lux's office, she headed straight for the café. Baking had become her form of stress relief, and lately she had baked plenty.

Granny Mae had taken notice of the overflowing shelves in the display and had offered to take some things to the ladies at church, or Barbara Ann's salon down the street where she was certain Barbara's clients would love a cookie or two.

She had even heard Rosie's comment about "mixing the beaters right off that old mixer." There were plenty of people, including Leah, who had taken notice to the vibe that something was bothering her. Aside from the custody's visitation arrangements and her pregnancy, Rachel wasn't concerned with much else.

Leah and Willow had squeezed in a visit earlier in the day when Rachel had taken a short break from the third batch of brownies that morning.

"Are you sure you should be working all these crazy hours?" Leah had asked her. Her response had been a pretty simple and straightforward "I'm fine."

Honestly, it wasn't like her body wasn't used to all the baking. She'd bake until her feet were too swollen and sore to stand on, or until her belly got so big her back began hurting.

This wasn't her first pregnancy and she had a feeling it wouldn't be her last.

*a*dam wasn't too worried about Rachel's hours at the café. What had him worried, though, was what she had been bottling up since agreeing to visitations.

Pulling into Levy's, he knew that the kids were with Rachel at the café, helping her bake the last dozen or so of muffins needed for the school's Muffins with Mom event tomorrow.

"How's that baby of yours?" Adam asked Liam when he walked up to the counter. He could already see the wear and tear of having a little baby in the house—it was written all over Liam's face. Another few months and he'd be looking like he had no idea what sleep was. He couldn't wait.

"She's doing good. Up about every couple of hours to eat, and falls right back asleep." Liam wiped the countertop off and tossed the towel aside. "Hate to say it, but I miss having Megan around."

Ever since Conner came back home, Megan had picked up more and more hours at the station. Adam wasn't complaining, because it was giving him extra hours at home with his family. But it was obvious that with Megan doing extra hours at the department, Liam was struggling to fill the bar's hours.

"Speaking of which," Liam said, pulling up a chair alongside Adam. "You guys set a date yet? You guys can have the reception here if you'd like. No charge."

"How's that a 'speaking of which'?" Adam asked, chucking back his drink. Setting an empty glass down, he looked at Liam and said, "To tell you the truth? We haven't. We haven't even talked about a wedding at all. We've been trying to get through one thing at a time. Taking it one day at a time. Starting this weekend. Tomorrow in fact."

Liam refilled his drink and slid it across the bar to him. "I heard. Leah mentioned something about Scott getting visitations. How's Rach taking it?"

Tossing back the refill, Adam said, "So far so good. I'm sure the town can attest to that, since she's been baking nonstop. It's once she stops baking that we have something to worry about."

On that note, he offered Liam enough to pay for his drinks and have a tip left over, and headed home.

ARRIVING HOME JUST as Rachel and the kids pulled into the drive, Adam offered to help Rachel carry in the containers of muffins that she would take to the school tomorrow.

Tyler was excited to know that she'd be there eating muffins with him at his school. He had told Adam on numerous occasions that he was happy to have Rachel in his life. She was the best. Adam had agreed and would always agree with that.

She had come into their lives by the grace of God, who had finally answered his prayers of finding someone to fall in love with and raise Tyler with. It was just his luck that she had come into their lives when they needed each other more than ever. Being a single parent was difficult, but finding the right person to raise a family with was a heck of a lot more challenging.

Wrapping his arms around her as she set the plastic containers on the counter, he kissed the back of her neck. Her shoulders were tense, more than likely a factor caused by stress of what was coming tomorrow.

Gently pressing his thumbs into the tense muscles of her back, he didn't have to wait long for her to relax, melting into his hands. He slid a chair out and offered her to sit down. Usually it was the other way around, but it was his turn to cash in on some of his debt he owed her from all of those nights he had come home with tense and sore muscles, not wanting anything more than a good old back rub.

"I'm not sure I can go through with it," she whispered, low enough for the kids not to hear. "I know that everything will be okay. I know that she will be fine once she's there, but I just worry about the what ifs."

She had talked about the what ifs every night for the last couple of weeks. He had promised her there was nothing to worry about. Worrying never helped any situation. And the stress wasn't good for her or their baby. He had made her supper each night this week, offering her favorite Rocky Road ice cream—sometimes even before supper was cooked.

He didn't have to say it again. This time she recanted her statement, agreeing that she was probably worrying over nothing. "Scott isn't a bad guy," she said, leaning into his grip on her shoulders, silently begging him to go deeper with his thumbs. "He just wasn't the one."

Adam pressed his thumbs in deeper, concentrating on the knotted muscle. He didn't care to hear about Scott, but he had a feeling the guy would treat Ava like the princess she was. When a lot of other men would feel a hit to their pride, or defensive of their territory, he had stepped back and realized it was best for Ava to know her father. And hey, she got two dads out of the deal, so that was a plus for her.

"I'm sorry I keep talking about it," Rachel said, rolling her head around in a circle in an attempt to loosen the stiff muscles in her neck—the next place his thumbs would venture to, once the muscles in her shoulders and upper back gave way from the knots.

"You don't have to be sorry, Rach," he offered, massaging deep enough to cause a deep moan to escape off her lips. Hearing her moan like that caused things to heat up. One of the reasons he had concentrated on the muscles, and not the way she was reacting to the massage. "You shouldn't make those kinds of noises though. Unless you want me to haul your butt upstairs and leave the kids without supper for the night."

Laughing, she leaned forward, away from his grip. "How about after supper when the kids are in bed?"

Rubbing his hands along her neck, massaging the stiffness out, he agreed to take a raincheck for now. They had plenty of alone time once the kids were in bed. What they didn't have now was enough time to cook supper before their kids starved to death.

30

No one could have prepared her for the moment Scott picked Ava up and drove her away kicking and screaming in the back of his truck. He had promised Rachel that everything would be okay. He would take her to the park and possibly swimming, depending on the weather.

It sounded good, but not good enough when it was compared to those blood curdling screams coming from the backseat, as he drove down the road in the opposite direction of Cedar Valley.

It was lost on her what to do with herself once Ava was out of sight. She wanted to call Scott and make sure Ava was okay. Heck, she had put his phone number on speed dial just in case she needed to hear Ava's voice, or needed to tell her she loved her for the millionth time.

Adam had reassured her that Ava knew Scott. He had visited plenty of times, and that they were all sure Ava was comfortable with him being around. The fact that she didn't call him dad yet wasn't a justified reason to feel different about the situation.

She knew Adam was right, but what didn't settle her racing thoughts was the fact that Ava hadn't ever been without her for more than a day's time. Sure, she had stayed the night with her grandparents, but that didn't count. This time it was somewhere she wasn't used to.

"We saw his house, Rach," Adam reassured her once again. "He has everything she needs, including her favorite Sesame Street shows and Cheerios. She's going to have fun there."

The thought of waking up on Saturday morning without the sound of Ava's babbling and the tunes from Sesame Street echoing through the house, saddened her. The thought of missing their breakfast together, snuggling up on the couch for their afternoon nap, followed by the evening play outside in the pool with her swimming toys was enough to break her heart.

Adam's arms pulled her close. The smell of his cologne and the warmth of his body pressed against hers and caused her to release the breath she had been holding. Relying heavily on the sigh to make her feel better, she pressed against his chest and allowed him to comfort her as she lost control of the emotions she had tried so hard to overcome.

"It's okay," he whispered, guiding her up to the front porch, his embrace never losing contact with her as he sat down next to her on the swing. "Everything is going to be okay, I promise."

Finding comfort in his words, she leaned in closer to his chest, wrapped her arms around his waist, and allowed the scent of his cologne to linger in her senses for as long as she could.

There really was no one else she would rather be with than him. No one else she would rather spend the rest of her life with than with him. With Adam, everything felt right. Unlike the unsuccessful relationships in the past, this one brought a sense of familiarity, ease, and security.

She had been an emotional wreck for the last few days, and this man had stayed by her side, never faltering and never waning. When she had felt uncertain and full of doubt, he had been there to provide her with stability and the certainty that she was lacking.

Looking back at the time she debated on making the move to Cedar Valley, she had contemplated the pros and cons of doing so. Never once had she imagined that so much more would have been offered in her life, along with Ava's. She hadn't imagined a life rich in love and full of honesty and sincerity. A life filled with passion, desire, and a willingness to keep trying when the odds were against them.

Ava would be okay, just as Scott had promised. There would be nothing that man wouldn't do for his daughter. She knew it as well as anyone else knew it. She had no reason to worry. Worrying only robbed the happiness of the present day, or however her mother used to say it.

"Adam," she said, speaking loudly enough to wake him. He had gotten quiet sometime between her thoughts, and even though she would give anything to stay outside all night with him sitting on this swing, the night breeze was becoming chilly since the sun was setting low behind the mountains. "What do you say we head inside and watch a movie?"

She sat up as he adjusted in the swing behind her. "Just a movie? I thought you'd never ask."

They shared the laughter between themselves in the quiet night as they found their way across the porch to the front door. Each held the other tight; their bond with each other was full of warmth and love, without a single doubt they were meant to be together.

After climbing into warm pajamas, Rachel grabbed the king sized quilt off the back of the couch and sat down next to Adam. There weren't too many nights they had alone, and taking full advantage of every minute tonight was on the agenda.

"What movie were you thinking?"

Rachel tapped the side of her mouth with the tip of her finger as she looked across the room at the stack of movies they had to choose from. "I'm not really sure I was thinking of a movie, to be honest."

"Oh, really?" He turned to face her and pulled her close. "What'd you have in mind then?"

Getting into a comfy position, she nestled herself in his arms. She mentioned the thought she'd had of lying in his arms, talking about their future and how everything she needed had been right here in Cedar Valley this entire time. There was no denying the fact that true love existed and was easier to find when you weren't paying attention. Stumbling upon Adam was something Rachel would cherish forever.

"I love you, Adam Jacobsen."

"I love you, too Rach."

AFTERWORD

Love Christina and her books?

Sign up for her newsletter here: https://goo.gl/VeDPrm

Visit her website: www.authorcbutrum.wordpress.com

If you enjoyed Everything She Needed,
please leave a review on Amazon

ABOUT THE AUTHOR

Christina Butrum launched her writing career in 2015 with the release of The Fairshore Series.

Writing contemporary fiction, she brings realistic situations with swoon-worthy romance to the pages - allowing her readers to fall in love right along with the characters.

When isn't busy writing, Christina enjoys spending time with her family. Christina Butrum looks forward to publishing many more books for her readers to enjoy.

Connect Below!